Sharon & Larry

Love Found in Manhattan

By Marlene Worrall

Blessings & Joy

Marlene Worrall

ISBN-13: 978-1544813783
ISBN-10: 1544813783

DEDICATION

I would like to thank the following:

Teresa Lily, Jo-Anne Durgin, Cynthia Hickey, Ramona
Tucker, Ken Kuhiken, Lee Coryell, Linda White,
Michael Ireland, Don & Verneil Kallevig and Peter
Paras. .

Also thanks to the prayer warriors, you know who you
are.

Special thanks to my beloved sister, Verna, who
believed I could write before I began the journey.. .

Chapter One

"...Ms. Vandermeer...I'm sorry. The pilot and your parents were instantly killed. The Cessna 152 exploded on landing. Investigators are at the scene at LaGuardia searching for clues among the charred debris...hoping to determine the cause of the crash- a formidable task given the circumstances." Constable Rogers spoke softly and evenly, the gravity of the situation apparent in his tone of voice.

His voice was coming down a long tunnel. She closed the door behind the Constable and Cop in a daze. *Lord, no.....* Tiffany collapsed onto her yellow floral, chintz sofa. Clara, her adoptive mother, had helped her select it, along with everything else in her luxury Manhattan condo.

Tears tumbled down her cheeks. Silver, her Burmese cat, sprung onto her lap, sympathetic blue eyes searching hers. She pulled the feline closer to her bosom before setting him down. She couldn't breathe. She moved toward the terrace of her seventh floor apartment. She had to get out. She opened the door and was instantly slapped with a blast of freezing cold air stinging her face. She inhaled it and found her breath. Chunky snowflakes danced and swirled in a blurry white haze around her. Closing the door quickly, she located her cell and punched in the numbers for her best friend, Tracy Hamilton. "Something dreadful has happened..." She spilled her guts to her best friend.

"Oh, Tiffany, I'm so sorry. Words fail me... get on a plane and spend Christmas with us...oh...I guess you have to deal with the funeral and all that stuff. Okay...um...call David and Barbara at the church, they handle crisis care. They're wonderful. And Tiffany, we're here for you...call anytime, day or night, we'll talk...we'll pray. Meanwhile, we'll be praying for you. Count on it. You're never alone. God will carry you through this. Remember the poem "Footprints in the Sand?" I'll pray with Mom as soon as we're off the phone. Put all your trust in Him. Remember, He cares for you. Tiffany...call us anytime. As soon as you've made the arrangements, get on a plane and come here. I took holiday time, so I don't have to be back in New York until the 10th. Maybe try to get a leave of absence from your job and spend some time with us."

Tiffany crossed the living room to the hall closet and snatched up her Sable coat. Slipping into it, she reveled in its' toasty warmth. It had been a gift from her beloved adoptive father only last Christmas. How could she have known it would be their last Christmas together?

Tears tumbled down her cheeks as she waited for the elevator. Reaching the lobby, she nodded to Sammy, the head doorman, unable to speak. Numb. She turned her face away from him, walking briskly outside into the blustery weather. Frigid air stung her face. She pulled her woolen cap down further on her face and plucked the collar up on her fur. The brisk walk would clear her head and invigorate her. Snow on the sidewalks was compressed from pedestrians tromping it, but she had to be careful to avoid ice patches. Walking as rapidly as she dared, she strode cross-town on Fifty-Seventh heading toward Fifth Avenue and the shopping hub.

"Lord, help me through this deep valley." The prayer was a whisper mingled with a wrenching sob. *"The Lord giveth and the Lord taketh away. Praise be the name of the Lord."* The scripture popped into her mind. Yes, she would be thankful in all things, not just the blessings. *Thank-you, Lord, for the time I was given with my wonderful parents.*

She reached Fifth Avenue. Bergdorf's windows were

elaborately festive. The city pulsated with energy and the Christmas spirit. A couple, obviously in love, walked hand-in-hand, singing a carol. "Silver Bells, Silver Bells..."

Tiffany peered into the windows of FAO Schwartz, the legendary toy store. The window display featured a white tree with oodles of varying baubles, Christmas lights and dazzling ornaments. A glittering silver angel presided over the tree top. A variety of toys graced the windows, including dolls in festive outfits and a small group of cuddly Teddy Bears of varying sizes. A train set was in motion. A young boy pressed his face against the window. "Mommy, Mommy, buy me that train set!!! I want a train set!!" "Shush," the woman said. "Daddy and I already have your Christmas presents...but maybe Santa will bring it."

New Yorkers rushed and pushed to move along faster. But many folks were gay fueled by the Christmas Spirit. A group of traveling carolers, clad as old-fashioned villagers, gaily warbled Christmas carols in front of the store. *"Deck the halls with balls of holly, fah, la la la la la la la la."*

Tiffany strode briskly past the stores and hotels, most of which were flanked with soaring, brilliantly decorated Christmas trees. Throngs of people crowded the sidewalks, while others hurried into the stores. Children giggled as they pointed to toys in windows or tugged on their parents' coats, begging for one of the many gift suggestions displayed in the windows. Horns honked in the congested traffic, shoppers laden with gifts leaped in and out of taxis. The hustle and bustle of the Big Apple was at its apex. Christmas Eve was only hours away.

The snow fell in thick sheets. She walked beyond the frenzy of the shopping core with no destination in mind. The heavy snow blurred her vision. Suddenly, she realized she had walked into the seedy area of the West Side. "Ninth Avenue! I've walked too far from the city core," she said to no one in particular. As she turned to head back to the shopping district, a piercing scream of an infant stopped her in her tracks. She whirled around following the sound. But there were no Moms with babies anywhere to be seen. Still, the wailing continued. The sound seemed to be coming from the deserted alley. "Keep moving, Lady," a heavy-set surly man, barked. An older woman glanced in the direction of the wailing, but kept on moving like everyone else on the sidewalk.

Tiffany moved away from the crowded sidewalk, following the sound. Soon she stepped into the nearby alley. The heart-wrenching sobs of an infant caught at her heart. *That screaming is coming from...a trash can in the alley! It has to be!* Rushing toward a row of cans, she followed the wailing to one with the lid askew.

To let oxygen in? Snatching off the lid, she peered inside. Flabbergasted, she glimpsed a tiny, delicate infant. He gaped up at her, enormous blue eyes growing wider as tears streamed down his sweet, innocent face. He stopped screaming for a few seconds, squirmed uncomfortably and then continued wailing.

Carefully, Tiffany rolled the garbage can onto one side, gently scooping the infant into her arms. His blankets were luxurious, blue and felt soft like cashmere. *God sent me here. Someone must have just dropped him off. Though he's obviously traumatized, he seems unharmed.* "It's all right, darling. You're going to be just fine," Tiffany cooed, as the infant fussed and wailed, albeit less frantically. Cuddling him close to her body as she walked, he gradually began settling down. *Who would discard this precious infant? And why?*

With the baby snuggled in her arms, Tiffany pulled her cell from her purse and called a taxi, despite knowing the futility of it. Busy. Of course, it was Christmas Eve. It would be a long shot if she were able to get one at all. She smiled at the infant and felt tears of joy trickling down her cheeks. "You are so sweet...so precious. What's your name, Darling?" A maze of chunky snowflakes danced around them. She pulled the baby closer to the warmth of her fur coat and body.

The temperature had dropped again. Soon, it would be too cold to snow. The wind howled. She hugged the infant even closer to the toasty fur. *Lord,* please *send a taxi, quickly. The baby could freeze to death.* She hit "redial" on her cell every few minutes. Engaged. *No kidding. It's Christmas Eve. Getting a taxi anytime is a daunting challenge.*

Had the baby's mother or father planned to return for him in mere minutes? Surely his parents would know the infant would freeze to death or suffocate. Had the baby's life been in jeopardy? What would happen if she failed to report the missing infant to the police or authorities? If no news report cited a missing baby, she would be in the clear. *What was she thinking? That's crazy.* Only a desperado would have dumped the precious infant into a garbage bin. *Desperate or insane.* Maybe she'd better call the police. But she had to hold him just a teeny bit longer.

Someone had abandoned this infant just like she'd been abandoned when she'd been a toddler. She didn't want him to grow up in an orphanage like she had. Lord, if you would forgive me, maybe I will just keep this baby and raise him as my own.

She could easily afford him. When the estate was settled, she would be a wealthy woman. "Donnie," that's what I'll call him. She smiled down at him, leaned over and planted a kiss on one of his rosy cheeks. Vivid blue eyes stared up at her as though he accepted her as his new Mommy.

Reality was fast kicking in. She knew nothing about babies. Common sense dictated she should find a drug store and buy some baby basics. She would just have to wing it until she had a chance to Google it. "How old are you, Donnie. Six months?" He looked up at her with a smile. *Maybe this is your gift to me, Lord. After all, you move in mysterious ways.*

A taxi dropped off a couple across the street from where she trudged, carrying the infant. She whistled loud and shrill. The driver glanced in her direction, swung his taxi around and stopped. "Where to, Miss?"

"The drug store on Lexington and Sixty-third, please." She stepped into the taxi with the blue bundle snuggled in her arms.

"Sure, lady." He glanced both ways and pulled away from the curb. "That's some shrill whistle you have. I might not have spotted you if I hadn't heard it. "

"I grew up in New York."

The taxi crawled at a snail's pace cross-town on Fifty-seventh. Finally, the driver pulled up in front of the drug store. 'forty-six bucks, Ma'am. Tiffany gave him three twenties."Keep the change. Merry Christmas!" She loved being generous, especially this time of year. What was that scripture? *"Cast your bread upon the waters and after many days it shall be returned to you."*

"Thank-you, Ma'am! Much appreciated! Merry Christmas to you and your sweet baby!" He grinned as a couple ducked into his vacant cab.

New York-my favorite city in the whole world. I wouldn't trade it for anything. Tiffany held Donnie close to her chest. Holding him and knowing that he needed her, gave her life a whole new meaning. *She wouldn't be alone for Christmas, after all!*

Jason Prescott hadn't been sleeping well lately. In spite of the fact that he was a doctor, he wasn't big on medication. Didn't like sleeping pills-favored Melatonin. Natural herb products would help induce sleep. He'd been upset and unable to sleep ever since the ugly court battle.

Tiffany almost collided with him as they both entered the drug store at precisely the same instant. "Sorry Ma'am. I beg your pardon," Jason couldn't help but stare at the stunning young woman. She held a baby in her arms. *He had a weakness for redheads. This one had tilted, emerald eyes and porcelain skin. But she held an infant. Married, no doubt.*

Tiffany peered up at the man she barely avoided colliding with. Her heart skipped a beat. The stranger was tall and ruggedly handsome in an off-beat way.

He grinned down at her, his broad shoulders

practically bursting out of the sheepskin jacket he wore. His white turtleneck contrasted starkly with his olive or maybe tanned skin.

What a gorgeous hunk. I may be grieving but I'm not dead. The man must work out. She loved his wavy dark hair. It looked tousled or unruly-like he'd forgotten to comb it. *An absent-minded professor? He did look intellectual.*

"Sorry...I was...preoccupied with...the baby. I...I didn't mean to bump into you." A thrilling sensation soared through her body right down to her toes. *Chemistry? Oh yeah. The kind of chemistry she never knew existed.*

"Cute little guy." He grinned down at the baby, and shot a glance at her ring finger, which was bare. He peered at the infant. "Must be urgent...to bring you and your baby out in this weather...and on Christmas Eve."

"He...he's not my baby. I'm...just looking after him...for a sick girlfriend. *Lord...I...didn't mean to lie, I'm sorry... Why did she feel this enormous excitement just being in his presence? Was it just her? Or was the air charged with electricity? She'd heard about chemistry, but she hardly imagined something like this!* She took a deep breath. *The man was talking. Maybe... she should listen.*

Jason was grinning at the infant. Donnie gurgled and

squirmed. "Perhaps I can help. It will be awkward shopping with that infant in your arms."

"Well...I...guess that would be helpful...since I have to pick up several things." *I must be losing it. I don't know this man from Adam.* "He might start fussing, though. I don't think you would want to deal with that. Thanks, anyway." She turned away from him and tried, awkwardly, to push the shopping cart, while holding the infant.

"Come on. Let me help you. I'm real comfortable around babies. As it happens, I'm a doctor, an obstetrician."

Sure you are. What a line. She narrowed her eyes. "Really?"

He produced his ID, flashing it proudly. "I'm a brand-new doctor. I work at Cornell Medical Centre in pediatrics."

She glared at the ID. "Dr. Jason Wilcott." She hesitated a few moments. "Well...with those credentials...I...guess you're qualified to hold a baby." She smiled, in spite of herself. "Thanks."

He grinned at her. "And you are?"

"Tiffany Vandermeer. Nice to meet you. The...baby is my girlfriend's. She's...very sick..." A thrill zinged right through her and zapped straight down to her toes. *A thrill? Because a man grinned at her and wanted to help her with her shopping cart? Get a grip.*

11

She started piling items into the cart-a baby bottle, diapers, pabulum and other basics. A mixture of sadness tinged with hope washed over her. Tears trickled down her cheeks.

Jason glanced over at her. "Whatever is wrong? What has happened?" His face reflected genuine concern.

"My...my parents...they were...killed...in a plane crash...early this morning. I'm in...shock."

He moved closer to her. "How dreadful for you. I had a hunch something was terribly wrong when I first saw you. I just had this...feeling...that some sort of tragedy had befallen you. Let's get the shopping done - then I'll have my driver take you wherever you need to go."

"Oh no...I couldn't do that...I have to..." Her eyes welled up with tears, again."

"You're not going to be alone on Christmas Eve - not if I can help it. You need a shoulder to cry on." He grinned. "I have broad shoulders."

"So I see." She stifled a giggle... or was it the onslaught of hysteria?

Jason selected a few baby items also, to add to the growing pile in the cart. He surveyed the items they had chosen. "I think that pretty much does, it, don't you?" He looked to her for confirmation.

"Yes, I think it does."

"Don't you need a stroller or baby carriage?"

"Yes, I guess I do." *A sense of normality was beginning to return to her.*

"I walked here, because I only live a few blocks away," Jason said. "But with the baby and all, I'll call my chauffeur and he'll pick us up and drive us to Bloomingdale's. We'll stay inside where it's warm until he drives up."

"I couldn't possibly put you to that trouble, Jason."

"Drug store, Lexington and 63rd Nick. We'll watch for you." Jason talked on his cell making the arrangements. He finished the call. "Of course you can. That's what friends are for."

Tiffany and Jason stood in the lineup for the cashier. A jolly sales clerk wearing a red hat trimmed in white, tallied up the items."145.80, please Ma'am. Oh, what a precious baby!" she cooed. "You lucky girl," she added, as Tiffany slid her credit card over the machine. "Merry, Merry Merry!" The clerk smiled as she sang her own version of a Christmas greeting.

Silver Bells was playing in the store. Many of the customers were singing or humming along with music. *Her folks were in a better place. And maybe this Christmas would turn out to be truly amazing.*

Before Tiffany could think of a reason to protest, Jason gestured for her to join him. "He's already here." Jason set the shopping bags down and opened the door for her. "Hey, Nick, take us to Bloomingdales, would you?" He glanced at Tiffany. "Tiffany, say hello to my driver, Nick Farentino. Nick, meet the lovely Tiffany Vandermeer and Donnie, her girlfriend's baby."

"Nice ta' meet ya," Nick said, hurrying to help Tiffany onto the leather seats in the back of the limo. Jason slid in next to her, stashing the shopping bags on the spacious floor. "Traffic is at a standstill. It will take us longer to get there than if we'd walked, but I didn't want to chance either of us slipping while holding the baby."

Nick skillfully maneuvered the limo away from the curb and into a traffic lane as slush splattered the vehicle and the sidewalk. They crawled at a snail's pace, finally arriving at the famous department store, almost a half hour later. Jason helped Tiffany and Donnie out of the limo.

Bloomingdale's bustled with activity and excitement as the clock raced toward Christmas Eve. Last-minute shoppers scurried around the busy store, clutching brightly-colored shopping bags. Others waited in line for cashiers. *Thank you, Lord, for sending this wonderful man and this darling baby to assuage my sorrow. I know how much you love me. Thank you, precious savior.*

"Here we are. Fifth floor, Baby carriages" Jason announced.

They stepped off the elevator and walked onto the floor, which was crowded with merchandise. "There they are," Tiffany said, pointing across the room, as she spotted the baby carriages. They strode over to the strollers and carriages. "Is that stroller collapsible, Ma'am?" Jason asked the clerk.

The mature, harried saleswoman hovered near them. "It sure is. You want to take it with you? Or would you like it delivered?"

"We'll take it with us. I also need a collapsible baby carriage. Which one do you recommend?"

She guided them over to one. "This is our most popular model, Ma'am."

"I'll take it," Tiffany said, barely glancing at it.

"You're a fast shopper, Tiffany. I'm impressed." Jason grinned approvingly, as they rode the elevator with their new purchases, down to the main floor.

Her heart lurched. It almost felt like they were a married couple and this was their baby.

"Why don't you consider changing your mind about tonight? Mom said she was flying in from Palm Beach, but she cancelled out at the last minute. I managed to get a few days off, thinking I would spend some quality time with her. Instead, I'll be alone."

"Why did she change her mind?"

"I think it has something to do with the new man in her life. Ever since Dad died, she's been kind of scattered."

"I see. Well, let me think about it. I feel like I just want to be alone and grieve. I'm sure you understand," Tiffany said.

"Don't think too long. Christmas Eve is tonight."

She smiled at him. "So who were *you* planning to spend Christmas Eve with, once you realized your Mom wasn't joining you?"

His eyes twinkled. "You. Maybe God put you in my path so I could take care of you. I really don't think you should be alone tonight. Anyway, I'll bet your folks - if they knew you had a chance to celebrate Christmas and help a lonely bachelor through the season...well, I bet they'd tell you to be a Good Samaritan and do it."

She smiled through her tears, and for that moment, the sorrow lodged inside of her was stilled.

"You would be the highlight of the season. You and Donny will be my honored guests for Christmas Eve dinner tonight and turkey with all the trimmings for Christmas dinner tomorrow. Our live-in cook, Maria, is originally from Sicily, and let me tell you - that woman knows how to cook."

Her heart lurched. It was a blessing to be invited somewhere for Christmas Eve since it wouldn't be spent with her folks. And it was good to have a new man in her life...a bonus that he was brimming with tenderness and compassion. *Lord, did you set this whole thing up?* She smiled heavenward. It was going to take a very long time to recover from her devastating loss. Maybe God was giving her a chance to catch her breath. She glanced over at Jason. "Well, since you put it that way...maybe I'll reconsider."

"We'll be pulling up to the front of your building in a few minutes. Why don't I ask Nick to wait out front? I'll help you with the crib and shopping bags." He winked at her. "Then, maybe you'll change into a festive outfit and come home with me. You really shouldn't be alone at a time like this."

"It would be nice not to have to spend Christmas Eve alone...with only a baby for company." Donnie started fusing. Common sense kicked in. *I better get home, sterilize the nipple and warm him up some milk. Lord knows when he was last fed.*

A motto from "Auntie Mame," one of her favorite films, popped into her mind." Life *is a banquet and most poor suckers are starving to death."* Yes, life was meant to be lived and enjoyed to the fullest. There was nothing to be gained by sitting at home alone. She would mourn her parents' passing - but right now she needed to survive emotionally through this Christmas season. Her parents would want her to spend Christmas Eve with someone. *Maybe God really had arranged this meeting so she wouldn't have to spend Christmas alone.* "Alright, Jason, you win."

"I'm so glad you came to your senses." He leaned over and planted a peck on her cheek. She whirled toward him. "What..."

He grinned, sheepishly. "I'm sorry, gorgeous. I...just find you so darn attractive..."

Ditto, she was thinking. But she didn't want to say it, so she just smiled back at him. "Don't let it happen again," she teased.

Traffic was insane as always. The limo crawled slowly, finally reaching her building, which was only four blocks from Bloomingdale's. Nick parked under the blue canopy directly in front of her building. "I'll leave the stroller in the limo, and help you take the collapsible crib up to your apartment," Jason said. The threesome entered the lobby. The doorman did a double-take but didn't comment on the baby. "Good-evening, Miss Vandermeer. And Merry Christmas."

Soon they were riding the elevator to her apartment. She set the shopping bags down on the living room table. "I'll wait downstairs and give you some space," Jason said, turning to leave. "Or, maybe I should keep an eye on Donnie, while you dress for dinner."

"So, I guess I'm joining you, am I?" She was grateful he was making decisions for her, because she felt immobilized, as the reality of this morning's horror flashed through her mind. "Thanks. That would be great if you could stay with Donnie. It would speed things up."

She closed the door to her apartment, plucked Donnie up out of the crib and held him close to her breast. Tears tumbled down her cheeks. She whispered to him. *"Thank-you, Lord, for sending Donnie and Jason to me. I know you're watching over me."*

She quickly sterilized the nipple for the baby bottle and warmed up some milk. "There you are, my little darling. Mommy loves you...and so does Auntie Tiffany." *How quickly she was settling into her new role as "Mommy."*

Jason turned on the TV and held Donnie, cooing to him, while Tiffany headed into her bedroom, glancing quickly through her closet to make a choice for tonight's dinner. She settled on a long, black skirt and glitzy gold top. Next, she moved into her dressing room and opened an ornate Jewelry box, brimming with precious pieces. She slipped on her emerald ring and put on the matching earrings. A quick brush of her flaming red locks, and Viola! She was ready to celebrate Christmas with her two new male friends. *Thank-you, Lord. You are truly a God of miracles.*

Nick opened the back door of the limo and helped her settle onto the seat with Donnie." We're on our way, gorgeous." Jason grinned over at her. Nick crawled along in the congested traffic. He was stalled completely much of the time. Finally, he pulled up in front of an elegant Brownstone at Madison and sixty-seventh.

"Home, sweet home," Jason chirped, stepping out of the limo and helping Tiffany and Donnie onto the street. Nick hurried around to the back to see if he could help. "We're good," Jason said, starting to lead the way up the sidewalk, which had been shoveled, leaving a nice pathway.

The Brownstone stood proud and stately adjacent to similar grand homes. "Nice place," Tiffany said, glancing toward it. The low iron fence cordoned it off from the street and adjacent homes. The houses were worth a fortune in today's market. *Old money, no doubt.* Her parents' townhouse, which she would soon legally inherit, was a mere eight blocks from here. It was not quite as posh.

"Tiffany, my dear friend Maria," he said. "Maria, say hello to Tiffany Vandermeer and Donnie."

"What an angel," Maria cooed, leaning down toward the baby as she greeted them in the hallway.

Donnie's face lit up with a sweet smile. He started making gurgling sounds. *Was I ever that cute?*

"How old is he?" Maria asked.

Tiffany had to scramble to answer the question. It made her nervous. "He's about...six months old. I'm not sure of the exact date that... my girlfriend gave birth to him. She's very ill...in hospital."

"What a sweetheart. I love babies... though I never had any." She pursed her lips in a fake kiss. "What hospital is your girlfriend in?" Maria asked.

Tiffany got the feeling she wanted to pick him up and hold him though she made no attempt to do so.

"She's...in Lennox Hill Hospital." *Lord, I'm sorry to let you down. I'm sorry for lying...please help me figure this thing out. Please don't let Jason find out.*

"Are you expecting other guests, as well?" Tiffany asked Maria.

"Joanna Prescott, Jason's Mom called to say she couldn't make it. Jason insists that Nick and I join y'all. He considers us family and vice versa. Do you have any family in town?" Maria asked.

A tear trickled down Tiffany's cheeks. "I usually spend Christmas Eve with my folks, but..."

"What's wrong, dear? You seem terribly upset." They had moved from the hallway into the living room. Maria guided her toward the sofa. "And what about your friend? Do you want to leave Donnie here and visit her later this evening?"

"No. She...she's not allowed visitors...she's in intensive care...and undergoing some tests...the nurse promised to phone me as soon as I can visit."

Lord, what am I doing? Packing one lie on top of the next. But I can't let Donnie out of my sight. What if he winds up in an orphanage like I did?

Tiffany turned her face away. She was glad she'd had a good cry in private. She wanted to be as composed as possible for Christmas Eve with her charming, new doctor-friend.

"Tiffany just lost her folks to a tragic accident," Jason said, appearing rather suddenly." Their Cessna 52 crashed at LaGuardia early this morning."

"Oh...I'm so sorry. You poor darling." Maria put an arm around Tiffany. "What a tragedy. And just before Christmas. I'm sorry you have to go through all this. I'll brew some tea to calm your nerves. I'm so glad you're spending Christmas Eve with us. You probably felt like staying home and mourning, but maybe God wants us to comfort you. ..just try to relax," Maria said, steering her toward the white sofa.

Tiffany sunk down into the luxurious cushions and set Donnie next to her in his bassinet. *Lord, what I'm doing is wrong. I have no right to keep Donnie. But Lord, I just can't let him go! I just can't. Please don't ask me to.*

She glanced around the grand rooms. Like her building, this was pre-war, also. She glanced upwards at the towering ceilings. *A grand home...designed for a family of wealth and privilege.* Pale yellow walls showcased fine paintings. Across from the pair of peach-and-honey colored sofas stood an ornate, white marble fireplace; the focal point of the room. A blazing fire crackled from it. Holly boughs were strewn across the mantle. *Thank-you, Lord, for the privilege of sharing Christmas with these wonderful, new friends.* She recognized the intricate design of the mirror. It was a rare French antique.

"I'm so glad you could join us, Tiffany." Jason settled onto a wingback chair next to the sofa Tiffany occupied. His eyes swept over her with male appreciation.

It wasn't lost on her. Her heart fluttered. *Why does he make me feel like this...giddy and excited? I've never felt this way before in my life.*

Maria served Tiffany the tea, soon returning with a tray containing glasses of eggnog. Christmas music wafted through the room. Presley's inimitable voice, anointed and rich, rang out with "O Holy Night."

Donnie seemed remarkably content, considering the trauma he had just endured - a *testament to the resilience of the human spirit.* She glanced at Nick. A burly man, he had a shock of charcoal hair, graying at the temples and eyes that were dark and brooding. There was an air of tragedy about him. *I won't go there.*

"Eggnog, Nick?" Maria handed him one, without waiting for his reply.

"Thanks, Maria." His smile was genuine, his

countenance sad.

Tiffany glanced around the stately residence. A white, flocked tree flanked a corner of the living room. It stood near a bank of windows. Earlier, she'd noted the Christmas lights were visible from the street. Angel hair, multi-colored bells and trinkets, along with strings of twinkling lights encircled the tree, blinking off and on. *It's beginning to look a lot like Christmas* played in her head.

Donnie appeared to be fascinated by the vividly-lit tree. He kept stretching away from his bassinet to stare at it. Tiffany smiled at him. *What a darling boy. She was falling hopelessly in love with him.*

"Dinner is served." Maria announced, after about an hour. "I'll have my dinner in the kitchen. That way I can keep an eye on Donnie. I've warmed up his bottle."

Tiffany was amazed at the love they all showered upon her. "Thank-you, Maria."

The doorbell rang. Everyone exchanged glances. "Are you expecting another guest, Jason?" Maria asked.

"No, I'm not. But I'll see who's here." Jason strode to the front door. "Mother!"

"Well, darling, don't just stand there. Invite us in." She said, as Jason gestured his welcome. She carried a gold shopping bag with beautifully wrapped gifts inside it. "We decided to stop by on our way out to dinner. I didn't think you'd mind, darling." She smiled mischievously at her son.

"I'm glad you stopped over, Mother. What a nice surprise!" Jason said.

"Let me do the honors, darling. Meet my fiancé, Graham Saunders." She turned to Graham." My son, Jason." She glanced over at Tiffany, with a haughty air. "Oh... and who might this be?"

"Mother, may I present Tiffany Vandermeer. I believe you know everyone else. Tiffany, say hello to my mother, Joanna Prescott."

"A baby? Tiffany has a baby?" Mrs. Prescott glanced over at her, disapprovingly.

"It's not hers, Mom. She's looking after the baby for a sick girlfriend."

"A sick girlfriend? I see," she continued, haughtily. Joanna handed her Chinchilla coat and his black cashmere coat to Maria, who disappeared with them, returning to the living room quickly. "What can I bring you to drink?" She asked the new guests, unfazed.

"Well...what would you like, darling?" Joanna settled onto the loveseat and smiled over at her fiancé. Graham moved onto the loveseat next to Joanna. His personality perfectly meshed with the formal attire he wore. "A glass of Sherry might be nice."

Tiffany thought Graham was pompous. She could tell that Joanna was smitten with him.

Maria served the glasses of Sherry on a tray. Jason stacked more wood into the fireplace before taking a seat next to his Mom.

"Tell me, darling. How did you two meet?" Joanna lifted the glass to her lips, taking a healthy swig of the Sherry, as she glanced fleetingly in Tiffany's direction.

"Some other time, Mother. Tiffany's folks have just been killed in their Cessna 52. It crashed at LaGuardia this morning. She's hardly feeling social as you can well imagine. Still, I insisted she join us for Christmas Eve. I didn't want her to be home alone."

"I'm so sorry...but how does... the baby...fit in with all this..." Joanna Prescott arched an eyebrow.

"Some other time, Mother." His voice was stern. "Tiffany is hardly up to explaining things at the moment."

Thank-you Lord. And thank you, Jason, for protecting me. I can't handle your Mother's interrogation. You're absolutely right about that.

"Where are you staying, Mother?"

"We have separate suites at The Pierre, darling. The hotel owners are friends of mine. I'm sure you know that."

"Of course, Mother."

Tiffany was fascinated and intimidated by Jason's Mom. Raven black hair, beautifully coiffed, framed her classic face. High cheekbones and inquisitive hazel eyes gave her the regal look of a queen. She reminded Tiffany vaguely of Jackie Kennedy.

"Why don't you cancel your dinner reservations and dine with *us*, Mother?"

"Now, darling - where are your manners? That's would hardly be fair to Maria, would it? No, Jason, we've made *our* plans, and you've made *yours.* We'll be running along shortly." She glanced at her elegant, jeweled Cartier watch.

"Of course, Mother. Will I see you tomorrow?"

Joanna Prescott glanced over at Graham. "Quite possibly. What do you think, Graham? Maria is cooking a turkey with all the trimmings. She's a marvelous cook."

"Home cooking. Sounds irresistible."

"What time is Christmas dinner, Maria? We're thinking of joining the dinner party tomorrow, if you have enough turkey."

"There will be plenty. I'm cooking a twenty-five-pound turkey. Dinner will be served at 5:00."

"We'll be here." This time Joanna did not defer to Graham.

Joanna and Graham finished their Sherry. They rose simultaneously, as though it had been carefully orchestrated. "Darling, it was so nice to see you. Until tomorrow, then, dear." She planted a peck on Jason's cheek. Then, she glanced in Tiffany's direction.

"Tiffany, dear... so nice to meet you. Take good care of your baby, now, won't you." She flashed a parting smile as she regally strode toward the front door.

Tiffany smiled weakly. "Nice to meet you both."

Jason stood up, escorting his mother to the door. He glanced at Graham. "Excuse me, Graham. I'd like to have a private word with Mom."

"Of course. I'll wait in the limo," Graham said, moving toward the front door and their waiting car.

Jason lowered his voice. "Mother, I don't even want you to come to dinner tomorrow, if you can't behave yourself. No cheap shots at Tiffany, alright? She's been through enough with the sudden death of her folks. I happen to be very fond of her - even if I *have* just met her."

"Oh, really? Well, excuse me. I'll be sure to walk on eggs tomorrow." She glared at him. Then, softening, she kissed him on the cheek. "I love you, darling." She leaned toward him and whispered, teasingly, "Even if you do have poor taste in women."

He grinned and shook his head. "I love you, too, Mother. You better behave yourself, tomorrow."

I'll lead the way." Jason grinned, as he gestured for Tiffany to follow him. Opening leaded French doors, he ushered her into a stately dining room. He pulled out a chair for her at the guest of honor seat to his right, before seating himself at the head of the table. Marie made sure Donnie was settled in, placing the stroller next to Tiffany.

"I've made Cioppino with corn bread."

"Sounds delicious."

Tiffany smiled. She could hardly believe that's what was being served tonight. "It's one of my favorite dishes."

Maria set the bowls of Cioppino at the place settings, along with piping hot corn bread.

"I shall ask the blessing on the dinner," Jason said. He bowed his head and everyone followed his lead. "Lord, thank you for the meal set before us and the joy of having special guests for Christmas Eve. Bless our food and Maria, for preparing it. Amen."

"Now that's what Cioppino should taste like but rarely does," Nick said, after his first bite.

"It's delicious, Maria," Jason said.

Tiffany hadn't eaten a single morsel since she'd heard the shattering news this morning. She still didn't have much of an appetite. But the soup titillated her taste buds. She managed to eat some of it.

As she finished most of the small portion she had requested, she turned to Jason. "Why would an eligible bachelor be without a date on Christmas Eve?" The question had been nagging at her ever since she first met him. "I'm surprised you don't have a regular girlfriend, Jason. You don't strike me as a loner."

He hesitated before answering. "You're right. I'm not a loner. As it happens, I got involved with the wrong lady...she turned out to be a black widow."

"No kidding."

"A woman from Palm Beach - Brianna Moore - I met her at a dinner party...here in New York. She was a Palm Beach society hostess, and...I later learned... a black widow. Three husbands died under mysterious circumstances on her watch. Apparently she collected on the huge Life Insurance policies she had on them."

"She owns an opulent house overlooking the ocean in West Palm Beach. A few of her friends in New York and their guests were invited to attend a dinner party and be houseguests. I was one of them. A group of us flew in to West Palm Beach. Turns out, she was on a serious hunt for husband number four. When I told her I had no intentions of marrying her - this, after she pressured me into making that statement - she sued me for Breach-of-promise, asking me how I couldn't remember that I'd proposed to her. I was flabbergasted by her blatant lies. I had never proposed to her or even hinted at the possibility. In fact, I'd only taken her out a couple times before discovering her dubious past."

"I got a call from local hostess, Nancy Simpson, the following week. She had recently discovered some unsettling news about Brianna that she wanted to share with me. We had lunch together. I then learned what an unsavory character the woman was. It seems Brianna had done meticulous research and learned that I was from an old, moneyed New York family. That, coupled with my profession as a doctor, and the family's real estate holdings, was enough for her to throw the net out. I wasn't biting."

"She hired a Big-Guns attorney, and - incredibly - sued me for Breach-of-promise. Her attorney tried to pressure me into making an out-of-court settlement. I didn't rise to the bait. I must admit I'm more than a touch skeptical of women after that nasty fiasco. As a matter of fact, Tiffany - you're my first date since that horror show."

"Understandably. That's an outrageous scenario. What was the upshot?"

"It was thrown out of court for lack of evidence. Brianna was fuming. No doubt, she still had to pay her attorney's fees. After that nightmare, I swore off women for awhile. I have to say, if you weren't carrying that sweet, precious infant, we probably never would have met. I certainly would not have approached you."

God moves in mysterious ways. "You must love babies to have made a career choice to be an pediatrician."

"That's exactly right. I think it's the fact that babies are one of God's greatest miracles. Every time a newborn baby enters the world, and I hold the infant in my arms, I am freshly awestruck by our Creator."

CHAPTER TWO

The chauffeur pulled up in front of 300 East 57th Street. Jason accompanied Tiffany into the building. "Good-evening, Sammy." Tiffany said, addressing the doorman. Sammy looked mystified as Tiffany wheeled the baby in his stroller, into the lobby, her handsome beau close at her side. "Good evening, Miss Vandermeer. Merry Christmas," he said, practically choking on his words.

"Merry Christmas, Sammy." Tiffany handed him a generous cash gift, which was stuffed inside a Christmas card. This year's was nothing short of magnanimous. She absolutely adored giving to others. Her personal tragedy had made her appreciate their familiarity and ongoing kind and helpful deeds. Sammy's face lit up like a Christmas tree when he opened the envelope. She smiled at him. "You've been fabulous all year, Sammy. Thank-you. Seeing his delight was so worth the brief stop at a cash machine. She was heartbroken but rich - as the sole heiress of her parents' estate. And unless they had debts she didn't know about, she was about to become a very wealthy woman.

"I'm so sorry, Ms. Vanderbeen. I didn't want to pry when the cops came around, but I heard about the crash on the news. Let us know if there's anything we can do," Sammy said.

"You can pray that I'll have the strength to get through this. "Oh, meet Dr. Jason Prescott, and...the baby...is...someone I'm just looking after for a friend..." *That sounded like a fabrication, even to her own ears.*

Once the three of them were inside her apartment, Jason took control. He carried supplies into the kitchen, and started warming a bottle. "You just get dressed, Tiffany. And I'll take care of Donny. I know a thing or two about babies."

Tears slid down her cheeks. So much had happened so fast. And on Christmas Eve! She headed into her bedroom and glanced through her wardrobe. *Whatever I choose for Christmas Eve dinner should be gorgeous.* A stunning outfit jumped off the rack. *The black and gold dress...with my emerald earrings, necklace and ring I bought from an estate sale a few years go.* Her mind was on fast-forward. "I'll quit my *job. I'll need to stay home with Donnie and look after him. Beautiful, precious...darling, Donnie. She reflected on the discovery of him. He had barely cried when she picked him up. Strange, now that she thought about it - it was if an angel had led her straight to the infant. She never walked into that seedy area, and hadn't consciously gone there on Christmas Eve day. She'd been in a daze at the time. If only she could tell the police the truth and keep the baby. But she couldn't, of course. So she had to be very careful with whom she would share her precious secret.*

She loved this pre-war building with its spacious rooms, soaring ceilings and antique marble fireplace. It was far superior to the new condos in Manhattan with their cramped, modern rooms. As she put on the emerald studs, she reflected on the superb decor her Mom had masterminded. Her Mom's expertise and flair for decorating and selecting antiques had been instrumental in making her condo a glorious home to be proud of.

Her mom had been a gentle soul. A shrewd businesswoman, she'd always been a tower of strength and support for her. How would she ever get on without her? She could still hear her instructions: *"No, Tiffany, we need to inspect the antiques thoroughly before the auction. Once the auction is underway, there will be no time to mull things over. We don't want to get caught up in the frenzied activity. I'll make a list of the items we're interested in, and the top price we'll pay for them. That will be our modus operandi, and we must stick to it rigorously."*

She was grateful for the lessons she'd learned from her folks. Dad taught her diligence and discipline. He showed her how to research antiques thoroughly before making a bid. How she would miss him! Tears fell, unbidden. Suddenly, all the sorrow that had welled up during the day and early evening rushed, overflowing like Niagara Falls. She dabbed at her cheeks and quickly made her face up. Her crying might upset Donnie. She had to be strong. *Lord, please help me...and thank-you for sending Jason to me.* A scripture flashed through her mind. *"The Lord giveth and the Lord taketh away, praise be the name of the Lord."*

Tiffany emerged from her dressing room dressed to the nines. Jason paced around the apartment, Donnie in his arms. She peaked over at him. *No one will take this baby from me. Though her Mom had given her up for adoption, this child would be given everything money could buy and more love than he would ever know what to do with.*

"Ready Gorgeous?" Jason asked. His eyes swept over her from head to toe, lingering on her eyes.

Donnie stared up at Tiffany, enormous, vivid blue

eyes sparkling with delight. She turned to mush.

She took a whiff of the fresh, red roses before opening the miniature envelope. "For a very special lady. Enjoy the flowers. I'm praying for you." Jason's phone number was printed on the card. *God had shown up in her darkest hour.*

She plucked a crystal vase from her cupboard, filled it with warm water and emptied the floral preservative into it, arranging the flowers. She stood back, admiring them. "Gorgeous." She picked up her cell from the kitchen counter and dialed the number on the card. "Thank you, Jason. The flowers are just beautiful!"

"Beautiful flowers for a beautiful lady. You *are* joining us for Christmas dinner, aren't you?"

"I...I don't know." *After that last fiasco with Chad, she had sworn off men.* She couldn't get serious with Jason anyway, because she couldn't conceive. The man loved children. That much was obvious. Oh, she'd prayed off and on for a miracle. But presently, that was her condition. "Mind if I call you later? Donnie is...acting up."

"We'll pick you up tomorrow."

She hung up the phone. She *did* want to spend Christmas day with him, even if it meant being scrutinized by Joanna.

She snuggled onto the sofa, holding Donnie close to

her breast. *Jason. She couldn't seem to get him off her mind.*

Donnie suddenly started screaming. *Post-traumatic stress syndrome?* Knowing a doctor was certainly going to come in handy. *Why should his screams surprise her? The baby had been traumatized by the horrendous ordeal of being abandoned. How long had he been in the garbage bin before she'd stumbled upon him?*

She held Donny tightly to her breast. Her entire life was about to change. She was ready for it. Her mind flashed back to her encounter with Donnie in the alley. Donnie's Mom had wanted him to survive. Why else would she have left the lid of the garbage can askew, allowing air to flow into it? Also, he was wrapped in fresh, new blankets. *Had Donny's Mom been praying the right person would find him? Had she been keeping a prayer vigil?*

There were so many unanswered questions. Had Donny's Mom been married to an abusive man that had caused this desperate choice? Had the baby's life been threatened? Had the mother stuffed the infant into the garbage can with the idea of returning later to retrieve him? *Maybe she better fess up to the police. The thought gave her chills. If they found the real mother, and the infant was returned to her, what horrible fate might await this innocent infant?*

In the cold light of day, she had second thoughts

about it. *Did she really want to live a lie?* As it stood, she would have to concoct a fantastic tale and stick to it religiously. *Would there be an ad in the newspaper - a plea to have the baby returned to its' mother?* A flurry of thoughts ricocheted through her brain, unsettling her.

First things first. She warmed up some milk for Donnie, smothered him with kisses and affection, gave him a sponge bath, changed his diapers and put a new yellow cashmere blanket over him. *Thank God for Jason and Bloomingdale's.*

She opened her Bible and began reading. She kept it on her desk in the den. It fell open to the Psalms...*Was the Lord speaking to her? Should she do the right thing and report the infant to the authorities? Or was it already too late? She had bonded with Donnie and it was mutual....she felt it somewhere deep in her gut. The baby needed her desperately. And, oddly, considering the deplorable circumstances in which she had discovered the infant, he seemed relatively unaffected by the abandonment. She wondered why that was.*

A million unanswered questions swirled around in her brain. She had been brought up in the church by her parents. Taught to do the right thing in every situation. *Could she really live a life of deceit?* Maybe it wasn't about Donny. Maybe it was about her. Maybe *she* could not face life with no one close to her - no one to love.

Flashback. She was four years old and living with a group of other toddlers at an orphanage. It was sterile and cold, emotionally and physically. She shivered, even now, thinking about it. At night, she cried herself to sleep. She dreamed of having someone to love her, to hold her. "When will I get a Mommy and Daddy? Daily she pleaded with her caretakers. No, she couldn't give Donnie up. *She would never give him up. She couldn't chance having this precious baby end up in an orphanage.*

She opened her Bible and began reading and praying the Psalms aloud, seeking God. After some time, she felt that God was showing her that she should protect the baby from his Mom. Perhaps she was a heroin or coke addict.

She scooped up the innocent infant as he slept. He looked so peaceful snuggled beneath the cashmere blankets. She held him close. He stirred but did not awaken. *He's content.* Thank-you, Lord, for this precious gift. He probably would have frozen to death if she hadn't found him when she did. *Surely an angel had directed her to him.*

Thou shalt not steal. Would taking this baby classify her as a thief? Or was he a savior? Maybe the mother didn't want to be identified... perhaps for some sinister reason. Had the baby's life been in danger? Had someone wanted the baby to die? Or had the Mother prayed someone would find him? Something drastic had driven the baby's mother or someone to stuff him into the garbage bin.

She'd kicked around the idea in her mind, but she really did not want to go public, in case it put the baby and herself in danger - maybe the mother, as well. *In fact, if she was smart, she would stay out of the public eye for awhile.*

Reality began to kick in. She would be completely tied down by the infant. She would need a doctor to check the baby's health and determine if he had any special needs or medical problems...and she just happened to know one. Taking care of an infant was something she wasn't prepared for. She remembered what her vocal teacher had said. *"Inch by inch everything's a cinch."* She was counting on that.

For one brief moment, she thought about giving the baby up, calling the police and getting her life back. *What life?* Her folks were gone. She was alone and she loathed her advertising job. Quitting it would be a relief. She'd send her boss an e-mail with her resignation right after the New Year.

Now that she was a mother and an heiress, and would be quitting her job, she could look around for some work that would interest her. Maybe try to write

TV commercials.

"Gurgle, gurgle." Vivid blue eyes gaped at her, as one of his small hands reached up to touch her face. *How sweet.* "How old are you, honey? Six months? Five? When is your birthday?" she cooed. "Tell you what, Donnie. I'm going to make one up. June third. How does that sound? Donnie smiled at her. "You're such a big, robust baby." Would *she ever meet his mother or father?* "I don't want to give you back. I'm already attached to you, Donnie." If only there was someone she could take into her confidence. *Her secret was bursting inside her.* "Do I dare share everything with Jason?" Donnie gurgled, gleefully.

She picked up the phone to call the minister at her church. But when she heard the recording she lost her nerve. *He would want me to do the right thing.* She fed Donnie some pabulum, changed his diapers and gave him his bottle. He settled into his crib.

"Jason, call me. I need to talk to you," she said aloud.

She flicked on the news. Apprehension rose in her gut. What if there was a report of an abandoned, missing baby? She listened to the news, her heart in her throat. Nothing. Thank God. *No one would be looking for Donnie.* "Are you giving me a green light, God? I sure hope so, because I feel like it's already too late to turn back."

Freshening up, she waited for the 11:00 news report, since there was no mention of an abandoned baby on the 10:00 P.M. news. If no one reported the missing baby today, she was probably out of the woods. She stayed riveted to the TV during the news. "A baby has gone missing from a... Manhattan Townhouse..."

Her heart stopped. *Would someone have taken the baby from the chic, upper East side and dropped him in a trash can in the run-down neighborhood where she'd found him? Why?* Her heart caught in her throat. She couldn't breathe.

"A two million dollar ransom has been demanded from the kidnappers for the safe return of the baby," the announcer said. "Kidnappers. Lord, is that it? Is that why the baby was wrapped warmly in clean blankets? But why put him in a trash can? Something could have happened to him."

"The five-year old girl goes by the name of Stacey. She has blonde, curly locks, brown eyes and was last seen wearing a red coat and making a snow-man in the back yard she vanished from."

Tiffany started breathing again. *Why did weird stuff always occur around the holiday season?* She picked Donnie up. "So many people feel alone during the holiday season. But we have each other, don't we, Donnie."

"It would tear my heart out to give him back, Lord. I don't think I can do it." *"The Lord giveth and the Lord taketh away. Praise be the name of the Lord."* Tears trickled down her cheeks. "My parents are in Paradise with you, Lord. Please let me keep Donny. I couldn't bear to lose him, too."

"We've bonded, haven't we, sweetheart? She kissed the infant on one of his cheeks. "Good-night, sweet darlin'. I'm close by, if you need me." His baby blues peered intently at her. "It's almost like you understand what I'm saying, Donnie."

Her ground line rang. She hurried toward the phone on her Louis Fifteenth desk. *Jason Prescott* flashed on the screen. She picked up the receiver. "I just wanted you to know, Tiffany - I'll help you with the funeral arrangements and everything else you need to take care of. You don't have to go through this alone."

Was he a mind reader? "That is really good to know, because I've made a list of some of the things I have to do... and honestly..." Tears sprung to her eyes. "I...wouldn't be able to handle it alone. Thank God for you, Jason." *The steps of a righteous man are ordered by the Lord.* It was not an accident she'd met Jason the same day she lost her folks.

She fell sound asleep dreaming of her new life with Donnie...and Jason.

CHAPTER THREE

She awakened early to the squeals of Donnie fussing and squirming. She picked him up in her arms, changed him and warmed a bottle for him.

Three o'clock finally rolled around. Glancing down to the street from her seventh-floor vantage point, she watched the long, black limo pull up in front of her building. It was likely Jason and his driver, though she couldn't be sure. There would be other limos pulling up on Christmas day, as well.

The intercom buzzed. She cast a quick glance in the hallway mirror at her outfit as she walked by. "I think he'll like this short, frilly red dress with my new suede pumps," she said to the mirror

"Jason Prescott is here," Sammy announced.

"Send him up, please, Sammy."

In minutes, there was a knock at her door. Tiffany opened it. Jason looked even more handsome than she'd remembered. Cocoa brown eyes flashed at her. His grin showed a perfect set of white teeth. "Merry Christmas, gorgeous." His red cashmere turtleneck peaked out from a black cashmere coat.

"Merry Christmas to you," Tiffany cooed. She wanted him to take her in his arms. His presence reeked of virility, power and a hundred other attributes. He sure smelled good. *Oh Lord, help me. My knees feel like they could buckle. He sure sets my heart to dancing.*

His eyes swept over her, drinking her in. "Hey, let me carry the baby. I'm good with babies, remember?"

Her toes started to curl. *A baby doctor. I think I can trust him to carry Donny*

The driver pulled up in front of Jason's Brownstone. The elegant entrance was flanked by a low, wrought iron fence. Masses of Christmas lights were visible from the open window as they climbed the stairs together. Jason pulled out his keys from his jacket pocket and opened the wrought iron gate, leading to the steps of the three-story home. He looked somewhat awkward, as Donny wriggled around in his arms. *Imagine that,* Tiffany stifled a giggle.

"My folks' co-op is on Fifth Avenue. It will be going up for sale. No children are allowed in the building."

"The rules and regulations of New York co-ops are outrageous. You have to be almost perfect to buy one-not to mention rich."

"Merry Christmas!" Maria's eyes danced, as she joyfully greeted her guests. She was dressed festively in a red sweater and long black skirt.

"Merry Christmas to you! That turkey smells delicious. May I have a peak?" Jason asked.

"Of course. I've made mushroom and oyster dressing, candied yams and cranberry sauce. Plus, I whipped up some Christmas pudding with brandy sauce for dessert."

"It sounds wonderful. I rarely cook. Mom usually cooked the turkey." Tiffany turned her face away, fighting tears.

Maria put her arms around Tiffany. "I've been praying for you, dear. This must be so hard for you. Just trust in the Lord. He'll take you through this. Remember his promises. *I will never leave you or forsake you,"* is one of my favorites.

Tiffany carried Donny into the living room after dinner. Jason settled next to them on the sofa. "There's a classic movie on tonight you might enjoy."

"What's it called?"

"It happened on Fifth Avenue."

"What's it about?"

"A homeless man moves into a mansion on Fifth Avenue while the owners are away for the winter. I won't give away any more details because I don't want to spoil the story for you."

"Sounds intriguing. I love the old classics."

"Me, too."

"There's so much gratuitous violence and bad language in films today. Then we wonder why youngsters emulate that behavior. On principle, I don't watch them."

"I agree. I think people are hungry for wholesome love stories...or comedies. Movies started out as entertainment and now a lot of popular films portray negative, terrifying images that no one would want to have in real life. It's shocking the public pays to see that. It gets burned into their psyche. Garbage in - garbage out. Small wonder we have so much crime."

Jason clapped. "Well said. Remind me to take you to London where you can speak at Speakers' Corner."

"It just shows how deceived the average person is," Tiffany said.

"True. I guess people see the current films, seeking to entertain themselves...trying to fill the void caused by not knowing Jesus," Jason said.

"How very true," Tiffany nodded.

As if on cue, Donny fell asleep. Maria cleared the table and vanished into the kitchen.

"I feel as though I've known you a long time, Jason. I'm so comfortable with you."

"It feels that way to me, too." Jason's arm was

around Tiffany, as they sat together on the sofa. "Don't you just love hearing Elvis Presley sing Christmas Carols," Jason said, rhetorically. "Tell me, Tiffany, what hospital is your girlfriend in?"

She hated lying. It went against everything she believed in. *Why did he have to nail her on this so quickly? Couldn't he just let things be?*

"She has...cancer. She's in the Sloan-Ketterling hospital on...." *Oh, why couldn't she be truthful with him? Why did he insist on pinning her down so soon after they'd met?*

"What about her Mom? No siblings?"

"No...she's... alone." Tiffany's mind raced. "I phoned the hospital, but she still isn't allowed any visitors."

Tiffany was becoming increasingly uncomfortable. *Time to go home. Maybe I should run as fast and far from him as I possibly can. Of all the occupations on the planet, why did he have to be a doctor? He would easily be able to check on her fake girl-friend. But would he? Why had she agreed to this date? She should have just stayed home and taken care of her precious baby. Now she was probably seconds away from blowing her cover. And worse, maybe she would be charged with...whatever they charged a person with who kept an abandoned baby without reporting it.*

"Why do I get the feeling you're hiding something from me?" Jason leaned closer to her.

49

His earthy smell wafted through her nostrils. There was just a trace of a woodsy cologne emanating from him. She had to get away from him. "Why would I be hiding something from you?" She laughed, but even to *her* ears, it had an artificial ring to it.

"You tell me. How did your friend get the baby to you, since she was sick?"

"I...she..." It was no use. She couldn't pack one lie of top of another. She might as well confess her crime. The tears rolled down her cheeks. *The sudden death of my parents. That's it. She would plead temporary insanity.* Although she wasn't in a courtroom, she felt like she was.

He was holding the baby. She whirled and stared at him. "Okay! I'll tell you. You're determined to ferret out the truth. So, I'll tell you!"

"Well?"

"I...I found the baby in an alley. He was abandoned... lying in a garbage can...wrapped in a clean, blue blanket. I heard screaming that sounded as though it were coming from the garbage bin in the alley. I'd been wandering aimlessly, since learning the devastating news of my parents' death. I was in shock. As I walked by an alley on Ninth Ave, I heard the petrified screams of an infant. I rushed over to the bin where the cries seemed to be coming from. I opened the lid and peered inside, flabbergasted.

At the bottom of the bin, lay an infant, wrapped in a blue blanket. He was the sweetest, most darling baby boy I'd ever seen. I scooped him up and held him close to my breast. Instantly, he stopped crying. I was hooked. We bonded immediately. His big, blue eyes stared at me, trustingly, as though pleading with me to take care of him." Tiffany glanced at Jason, tears trickling down her cheeks, as she tried to gauge his reaction. "There! Are you happy now? I'm in big trouble, aren't I?"

Jason looked at her, stunned. "That is outrageous! What were you thinking? You should have notified the police, immediately!"

Tears stung her eyes. She broke down, sobbing. "I had no idea why he had been abandoned. At first, I was going to contact the police...but he quickly grew on me...and I...I just couldn't turn him over to strangers. We...bonded instantly."

"I'm phoning the police immediately. The longer you keep him, the more complicated it's going to become."

"What if they put me in jail?"

"I'll call my attorney before I make the call." He shook his head. "I can't believe you did this."

"My...my parents were just killed...in the plane crash. I haven't even buried them yet. I was grieving - in a state of shock. It was...temporary insanity...that's what it was!" She blurted that out and immediately knew it was the truth.

"It must have been. You strike me as a responsible, upstanding citizen. You *are*, aren't you?" His voice and mood softened, noticeably. "Yes. You were in a state of shock...not thinking straight... devastated by your parents' sudden death."

She couldn't hold back the onrush of tears a moment longer. "I was...and I am. It's only Donny that got me through all this...thinking about his needs, caring for him...peering into that sweet, trusting face."

"I'll get you out of this. But fair warning, my attorney will have a lot of tough questions."

"Who is your attorney?

"William Barrett, the second."

"Never heard of him."

"He's a high-powered attorney. One of New York's best. I'll get him on the phone."

"On Christmas day?"

"Yeah - on Christmas day. This can't wait."

She held Donny close to her bosom as she leaned back into the luxurious sofa, closing her eyes. Tears trickled down her checks. *What had she been thinking to meet this man and confide in him? Now the game was over. How could she live without Donny? Lord, please help me.*

"Maybe the attorney will cite post-traumatic stress

disorder - and maybe that is what you have." Jason said, looking at her tenderly. He put his arms around her. "You'll get through this...we'll get through this. Don't worry, I won't abandon you."

"Don't you see? I was adopted after my parents abandoned me, leaving me in an orphanage. It was horrible there. I cried myself to sleep every night. I wanted to die."

"I'm sorry you had to go through all that. I've been blessed to have caring folks. Dad died four years ago. Mom moved to Florida. I remained in the house keeping Maria and Nick on. I inherited a couple million from Dad, but Mom owns the house, I pay rent to her."

"So, you know what it is to lose a parent, prematurely."

"I do."

"You have the most beautiful green eyes I've ever seen." Jason peered deeply into them. "What nationality are you?"

"Norwegian. Both my folks were from Haugasund, Norway."

"Were you an only child, too?" Jason asked.

"I was. Mom divorced Dad when I was three. He was a tyrant. Ultimately it drove Mom over the edge. She couldn't look after me, so I was taken to an orphanage. Then, just as Mom was recovering from the breakdown...I was around five...she said she was coming to pick me up and take care of me...tragically, she died of an overdose of medication before she was able to get me."

"That must have been traumatic for you. Was it ever proven that your Mom died of a medical mistake?"

"No. I tried to delve into it when I was about twenty. I didn't get very far. I was blocked at every turn."

"Hospitals have powerful legal departments. It's virtually impossible to lodge a successful lawsuit against them."

"So I discovered."

"When were you adopted?

"I was six. I loved my adoptive parents from the moment I met them. They were crazy about me, too. We bonded and had a wonderful relationship. We had our challenges like every family, but we got through them with God's help."

"Oh...there's my ground line. I'll put it on the speaker phone, so you can hear the conversation, Tiffany."

"Hey Buddy, how are you? Happy New Year."

"Something tells me you didn't just call to wish me Merry Christmas."

"Good instincts. I need your help, buddy. It's an urgent matter...I'd like to set up a meeting with you and my lady friend, as soon as possible. Any chance you could stop over here...right away? She's here with me."

"It's going to cost you...I'm booked off over the holidays. If I work, the fees are double....but for you and your lady friend...I'll bill at my regular rates."

"Thanks, pal. Nine hundred an hour, right?"

"It's a bargain really."

Jason stifled a laugh as he hung up the receiver. He glanced over at Tiffany. "The money will be a pittance if he can get you off, Tiffany."

CHAPTER FOUR

"How about some tea? I'll get Maria to brew some for us."

"Sounds good." Her hands were shaking. No way could she give up Donny. *What had she been thinking to accept Jason's dinner invitation? Maybe the problem was that she really hadn't been thinking clearly since the plane crash.*

Maria served tea with dark fruit Christmas cake. "Joanne and Graham had to head off to have dessert with some friends. Knowing Joanne, she would have only taken a small sample anyway. She confided in me that she stays slim by eating half of everything. Me? I like a good portion of everything. So I have a few extra pounds on me, I enjoy life." She cut a few slices and left plates and napkins on the coffee table.

Tiffany took a piece of the cake. She'd always had a sweet tooth and Christmas cake was one of her favorites. *She might as well enjoy it. Prison food would be dreadful. No, that wasn't right. She had to believe God for a good outcome. The high-powered attorney would get her off. Wouldn't he?*

She changed Donny and put him down next to her on the sofa, sticking a nipple into his mouth. The small gadget did wonders to soothe him. Her eyes swept over him, love and tenderness swelling in her heart. Tears trickled down her cheeks. She had bonded with him. How could she bear to lose him? And for that matter, how would *he* survive it?

Donny's enormous sky-blue eyes stared trustingly into hers. *No! No! No! No!* She couldn't go through with this. She had to talk Jason out of it. But how? She knew his mind was made up. She shouldn't have accepted his dinner invitation. If she'd had more time to construct a better story, Jason might have bought it. She'd been caught off-guard and now it was too late.

Did she really want to live a lie? Doesn't God hate all liars?

The doorbell rang. Jason opened it, ushering in a tall, well-built man. He was bald and it looked like his nose had been broken but never reset.

"Tiffany, I'd like you to meet William Barrett, the second."

"Bill will be fine." The attorney grinned.

"This is my new friend, Tiffany Vandermeer."

The attorney grinned and stuck out his hand. Penetrating, intelligent, slate-grey eyes bore into hers. She had a sense that he knew volumes about her as he studied her intently.

Jason waved him toward a wingback chair. "Make yourself comfortable, my friend. Coffee? Or would you prefer a drink of some kind?"

Maria poked her head into the living room on cue. "What can I bring y'all?"

"Mineral water with lime would be good," Bill said.

"Tiffany, what would you like?"

"I'll have the same, thanks."

"Cute baby," Bill grinned as he leaned over the infant peering at him.

Maria disappeared and soon reappeared with a tray containing Pellegrino water, along with tall glasses and lime. She set it down on the long coffee table.

"Suppose you start at the beginning," Bill said, resuming his seat.

Tiffany glanced over at Jason as though he held all the answers.

"Go ahead, Tiffany. I know this is hard for you." Jason glanced at her and then back to the attorney. "Bill, Tiffany's folks were killed yesterday morning when their Cessna 52 crashed at LaGuardia. She was traumatized."

"I guess. Just...take it easy. Tell me what happened.

Why do I get the feeling that sweet baby is part of the story..."

"Real good instincts," Jason said.

Tiffany relayed the story including her mother's nervous breakdown. Bill listened attentively without interrupting.

"We'll claim Post-traumatic stress syndrome. You said your mom had a nervous breakdown. She must have had a fragile psyche, like you. Let me do some research. We might claim you've had a nervous breakdown. In a way you have, even though you may not have labeled it as such. I think the key here is that you came to your senses and reported the discovery of the baby only days after you found it."

Tiffany lost it then. "I...I don't think I could bear losing Donnie. He's all I have in the world..."

Jason put his arm around her. "You don't count *me*? I'm here for you."

"Thanks." Her heart skipped a beat. "I appreciate that." She glanced up at him. Their eyes locked. *Thank-you, Lord, for bringing Jason into my life.*

Suddenly, the baby let out an uncharacteristic wail. Tiffany reached over to him, swooping him into her arms like a mother eagle. "It's...almost as though he understands what we're discussing, isn't it?"

Jason glanced over at Donny. He had stopped wailing the instant Tiffany scooped him up. The infant smiled up at her, joy and admiration shining from his eyes.

"You have a point. The two of you have obviously bonded. No question about that. But you can't legally keep this baby, unfortunately." Bill turned to Jason. "You have a couple of possible defenses. We need to report this, sooner than later. What do you say, Jason?"

"I say we let the grieving daughter bury her parents. Get the funeral behind her and then we'll make the call. That will give you a chance to do some research and make sure you know what options are available," Jason said.

He's protecting me - looking after me. How endearing is that?

"I take it you *would* like to legally adopt the child. Is that correct?"

Tiffany sniffled. "Oh yes, very, very much. And...the finances aren't an issue. I won't need to work. I can devote myself to him."

"Okay. It can't hurt to try. You would feel a lot better if the baby was yours legally, wouldn't you?"

"I sure would" She held Donny close to her breast. "See, darling. God is helping us find a way to be together. I knew He heard my prayers." She cooed and cuddled him...every fiber of her being screaming with intense longing. She was born to be his Mother.

The hard-nosed lawyer raised his eyebrows. "God?"

"Yes, God." Tiffany smiled, radiantly. "He has heard my fervent prayers and He's working out a way for me to be able to keep Donny, after all."

"Well, I guess you and Jason are on the same page when it comes to God. Personally, I don't believe He exists."

"How can you look at a newborn baby and believe there is no God?

"I didn't say I had all the answers. I just said I didn't believe in the man in the sky."

"You will, when the judge hands me the baby with his blessings."

"Well, you're a positive thinker, that's for sure."

"It's more than that...much more than that."

The meeting was over. Time to head home. Tomorrow morning she would have to make the funeral arrangements. *Lord, please give me the grace to make it through all this. She was operating like a robot, barely facing her emotions. She needed to grieve. Really grieve.* She wanted to be alone with Him and read His Word, seek His face.

Tears tumbled down her cheeks. Tears of relief and joy. She felt the hand of God in this meeting. *He would find a way for her to keep Donnie." With God all things are possible"* She had the means to fight for him. *If the Lord allowed her to, she would take good care of him*

*and give him a privileged life. As long as his real
mother didn't suddenly show up and fight to get him
back, she had a wonderful future with her precious son.*

Her high-powered attorney would make it all
happen. She'd better tell Jason that money isn't an
issue. Now was a good time. "Jason...I just want you to
know that I'll be a wealthy woman once my parents'
estate is settled...so...attorney's fees and taking good
care of the baby isn't a problem."

"Your...your parents were wealthy?" Jason asked.

She heard mistrust in his voice. Uncertainty. *What
was his problem? She had had enough of him poking
his nose in her business for one day!*

"You're the sole benefactor on their insurance
policy?"

"Well, yes. I thought I told you I was an only child.
Of course, I'll inherit everything. I told you that they
owned a co-op, remember?"

He peered at her, skeptically. "You...mentioned you
were an only child...and you did say they owned a co-
op..."

"Well, then..." *Oh no, he's thinking foul play! What
is his problem? Does he actually think I had something
to do with the plane crash, in order to collect on a life
insurance policy? I've got to get away from him. He is
downright weird. I thought he was off-base when he
started delving into the baby situation, but now he's*

crossed the line. She stood up then. Defiant.

"I'd like your driver to take me home. Don't ever call me again. If that's how little you think of me, there is no chance for *any* kind of relationship. Ever!" She scooped up the baby and her tote bag and stomped to the front door.

"You have to understand that I don't trust woman after Brianna and the lawsuit..."

"Tough. Find yourself another girlfriend. *Do not* ever call me again. You got that. Oh, and I'll find my own lawyer. Your guy is okay, but I prefer working with a believer, so that we're both on the same wave length. Thanks for a lovely dinner and...thanks for the *huge* amount of confidence you've placed in me." She fought back the onrush of tears.

"Wait. I...I'm sorry. I told you I'm just recovering from a horrific experience with Brianna. I didn't mean to project issues onto you...don't run away from me, please. I'm so sorry. Give me another chance, Tiffany. Please."

She was crushed. "Have your driver drop me. I...I'll need to think about this." She whirled away from him and into the entrance hall. As she stood there, her body shook. Disappointment and anger threatened to overwhelm her.

Jason ran after her. He grinned sheepishly. "I'll ride with you and Nick."

They didn't talk during the short drive to her apartment. The sleek black limo cruised up to her building. "I'll see Tiffany to the door, Nick. I won't be long. Maybe ten minutes," He stepped out of the vehicle, and then took Tiffany's hand and helped her out.

She had calmed down considerably." Thank-you for a lovely dinner...and thank-you for having your attorney go through some options for me. I need to be alone with the Lord-I have a lot of decisions to make. This is a hard time for me."

"Please, let me see you to your door. I guess after I heard about the baby, for a brief moment, I thought I was dealing with a...wacko. But you're not. I'm crazy about you, Tiffany. Let me see you to your door."

She shrugged. "Suit yourself."

He pressed the button next to the elevator. "Just so you know, I'm not letting you get away. God has thrust you into my path. You need a friend, whether you think so or not."

The elevator door opened. Tiffany, with the baby in a stroller, stepped into it. Jason followed. "Please allow me to help you with the funeral arrangements. Between the grieving and Donny, I know you're on overload."

"I...I put a call into our pastor. But what with the holiday and everything, I haven't heard back."

They reached the seventh floor. The elevator door opened. "Why don't you get some more supplies for the baby and come on back first thing tomorrow. I'm not on duty and I'll help you make the funeral arrangements. I checked with Maria. She's crazy about Donnie. She said she would love to look after him while we make some calls from my office in the house."

"You would do all that for me?"

"That - and so much more." Jason grinned at her.

"I could use the emotional support. My two closest gal pals called me. They're both staying in Florida for another week. Can't say I blame them. They sent flowers. I guess they don't realize I need someone to hang out with during this crisis."

"They *did* throw out an invite to Florida, though. Maybe after we make the arrangements, I'll fly down there for a few days. Both sets of parents own homes in the same neighborhood."

"Where in Florida do they live?"

"Sarasota. Longboat Key."

"No way."

"You know it?"

"I grew up there."

"Come on."

"I did. My folks have a house there - an old Southern mansion. It's been in the family for a generation. Dad opened a cosmetic surgery centre in Sarasota. He did procedures at his New York clinic in the summer and surgeries at his clinic in Sarasota during the winter months. Actually, that's where we found Maria."

"Small world."

"Well, what do you say? You'll let me help you tomorrow?"

She melted as she peered into his gentle brown eyes. For a man his size, roughly six feet, she had never seen such broad shoulders. She was a sucker for a man with big shoulders and a tender heart. The few, vague memories she had of her biological father, were that of a man who was cold-hearted, ruthless, self-centered - the polar opposite of this doctor; a humanitarian to the core.

She opened the door to her apartment. "Come on in. I won't offer you a cup of tea because your driver is waiting. Come on inside for a few minutes, anyway." She felt warm and fuzzy just being in his presence.

"You're an antique collector. I noticed them last time I was here. You have some fine pieces." Jason glanced around the apartment, approval registering in his eyes.

"My dad's influence. You might know of him. He was a successful antique dealer. Rosh Vandermeer."

Jason reflected for a moment. "Rosh... I know

Rosh...or I knew him. Didn't he have that rare book shop...in the seventies...on the upper East Side?"

"He did. It was a hobby. Antiques were his livelihood." She turned her face as tears stung her eyes. The mere mention of his name sent a sadness soaring through her. She was still in shock. Her whole world had swung out of kilter with the plane crash. *Thank-you Lord, for sending Jason and Donnie into my life. I don't know how I would have survived without the comfort and companionship they've provided.*

Though she had delved into the Psalms and Proverbs, desperately seeking solace in her hour of sorrow, it was only after she diligently searched the back of her NIV Study Bible, that she found verses that directly ministered to her, regarding the traumatic loss of her beloved parents. *Nothing would ever be the same again.* Somehow, she had to go on without them. She would have to lean on *The Everlasting Arms.* Only *He* could see her through this dark valley.

CHAPTER FIVE

Tiffany awakened abruptly to the sound of Donnie fussing and wailing.

"What's the matter, sweetheart?" she cooed, stumbling out of bed, half-awake. It was still dark outside. She scooped Donnie into her arms before changing him and setting him back down into his crib. He was still crying as she padded into the kitchen to warm his milk and put on a pot of coffee.

She'd been honed on challenges since she was a toddler surviving in the orphanage. That sort of fate couldn't happen to Donnie. She would see to it.

She skipped breakfast again. No appetite. She focused her attention on Donnie's needs. Her ground line rang. *Who would be calling her at this hour?* She glanced at the call display and smiled as she saw Jason's number flash across the screen. She picked up the phone. *Why would he be calling her at this hour?*

"Good-morning, Jason."

"Did you sleep well, gorgeous?"

"I did, actually. I'm just chomping at the bit for 9:30 to arrive, so I can go on a shopping spree for Donnie."

"Right. And that's why I'm calling. I want to offer the limo at your service for the day. Nick will pick you up and wait in front of Bloomingdale's and take you wherever else you want to go. And, if I'm not being too pushy, I'd like to go shopping with you, because it's going to be awkward, shopping with a six-month-old infant."

"True enough. But...that's not necessary. I was going to call a cab..."

"Look, Tiffany You need some help. You can't do this alone. God doesn't expect you to do what you can't do. Let me give you a hand, okay?"

Tears tumbled down her cheeks. It *was* too much to handle. She desperately needed someone to help her. "I...I was hoping to be at Bloomingdale's when they opened at 9:30. And, yes...it would be awkward shopping with the baby..."

"We'll pick you up at 8:00. You'll have breakfast with Maria and I. I'm going shopping with you. I'll hold Donnie, while you make your selections."

"Well, maybe you're right."

"Of course, I'm right. Actually, why don't you let me ask Maria if she would be willing to baby- sit - then we can swoop through the store and get what you need much faster."

She was starting to come to her senses. This was a good, solid plan - far superior to her own. But she couldn't accept his help. He was moving too fast for her. She was starting to feel suffocated. She had to focus on taking care of Donny and getting through the funeral.

Don't look a gift-horse in the mouth. Mom's advice flashed into her mind. "Okay, Jason, you're on. I need all the help I can get right now. It sure would free me up, if Maria were to take Donny for a couple of hours."

"I'll get right back to you. Don't go away."

She laughed. *Like she planned to dart outside with a six-month old baby! Maybe this was the hand of God. People on earth are His hands and feet. If he sent Jason to her, maybe it was for several reasons.*

Five minutes on the dot, the phone rang again. "Hey, it's me. We're all set. Nick and I will pick you up at 8:00. We'll have breakfast at the house. You can brief Maria on Donnie and we'll be at Bloomingdale's when they open."

Tiffany hurried into the bathroom. She flicked on a few strokes of mascara and applied pink lipstick. "I'm good to go" she said into the mirror. Her heart raced. *She could hardly wait to see Jason.*

He was early. "Buzz-buzz." The intercom was

already ringing. It was barely 8:00. She depressed the intercom. "Tell him I'll be right down. No need to come up."

"Yes, Ma'am," Sammy said.

Tiffany, with Donnie bundled up in her arms, slipped in the back door of the limo. She caught Jason's eyes roving over her long legs as she moved onto the seat. She liked short skirts and knew the Manolo pumps she wore were flattering. Her legs appeared longer and more shapely when she wore them. They were worth every penny of their outrageous price tag.

She appreciated being appreciated. It had been too long between beaus - two years to be exact. Two years since Lance shattered her heart into a million pieces. She had vowed never to fall in love again. But Jason was special. He was tender and attentive. His concern for others seemed to bubble up inside him. *Few persons become doctors. It's a special calling.*

Breakfast was terrific. Maria whipped up a Spanish omelet, serving it with gourmet coffee and freshly-squeezed orange juice. She felt better already.

"Don't worry, Tiffany, I'll take good care of Donny," Maria said. She cooed and tickled him, and put a finger into his little hand. He held onto it. They had bonded. She knew he would be well looked after while they were out. *Would Maria consider being a baby-sitter at other times, also?*

The driver whisked them to Bloomingdales. "Look at that! Perfect timing! The doors are just opening," Jason said, as they stepped out of the car. "Let's take the elevator, it will be faster than the escalator," Jason said.

"Here we are," Jason announced, as they reached the third floor. A display board listing departments and their contents was on the wall of the elevator. Children's clothes, baby clothes and toys were listed on the fourth floor.

Tiffany filled the shopping cart so fast Jason's eyes could barely follow her. Blankets, clothes and toys soon filled the cart.

They lined up with the other shoppers. She even tossed a picture book and small teddy bear into the mix. A friendly woman with three toddlers stood in front of them in the lineup. She glanced at the contents of Tiffany's cart. "First one?" She smiled from Jason to Tiffany.

"Yes." He smirked and grinned at Tiffany. Then, he whispered to her. "We should be so lucky."

He warmed her heart and made her glad to be a woman.

"Mommy, Mommy, thank-you for the dolly," the little girl sang out the words as she clutched her Mom's hand.

Jason and Tiffany exchanged smiles.

"You like kids, don't you?" Tiffany said.

"Ya, I do. When you grow up as an only child, you dream of having siblings."

"Yes, I know all about it."

Tiffany plunked her American Express card on the counter to pay for the purchases. The clerk handed them each two shopping bags containing all the items.

The limo was waiting at the curb. They stepped into it.

Babies are a lot of work, and it's just beginning. Lord, I hope I haven't bitten off more than I can chew.

She filled her shopping cart so fast, Jason's eyes could barely follow her hands as she heaved item after item into the cart - from baby togs to blankets to a large variety of toys. She didn't bother to check price tags.

They stepped out onto the snow-laden streets, carrying their shopping bags. Nick hurried to their aid, helping them with the bags. "Good thing you're back. I've had some serious contenders for this parking spot."

They settled onto the back seat of the limo. It crawled through congested traffic.

CHAPTER SIX

Back in her own apartment, Tiffany joyfully unpacked the bags and acquainted Donnie with all kinds of toys and new items.

"Thank you, Lord, for this joy. It will help me get through the sadness of making funeral arrangements." *Everything I'm doing involves Jason. What happened to independence?*

She watched Donny in his crib. He looked so content." I can't begin to tell you how happy I am to have you in my life, Donnie," she coed, leaning down toward him. He smiled, his big blues twinkling. Somehow, he understood her.

Her cell phone rang. "Good-morning, beautiful." Jason's voice was rich and husky.

"Good morning to you, Jason."

"What time should we pick you up?"

"Uh...give me an hour."

"We'll be out front."

"You're sure you want to do this? You must have so many things to do on your day off."

"I do. But nothing is more important than my helping you with the funeral arrangements. Okay, so maybe I put a few things on the back burner - just until I finish helping you make the necessary arrangements."

"Well, thank-you. I *do* need a friend."

"I've been through some valleys myself. Life has a way of throwing nasty curve balls, just when everything seems to be going smoothly."

"True."

"See you in an hour."

"Isn't God good?" Tiffany planted joyful kisses on Donnie's cheeks. *How could she ever give him up? This wonderful, precious child. Surely God had given her this baby. There are no coincidences, only God-incidences...right, God?*

She bundled up Donny in a snazzy, blue jumpsuit and wrapped the new, yellow cashmere blanket around him. He was becoming more settled as time went on. *He probably loves the cashmere blanket.*

She hated to yank him out of his crib - but the funeral arrangements had to be made. Holding him in her arms, she strode to the window. It was still snowing. A long, sleek limo cruised slowly and stopped in front of her building. That will be Jason. In minutes, she was downstairs, stepping into the limo as Nick drove them to Jason's Brownstone.

"I'll take charge of Donnie," Maria said, as soon they were in the house. "I know you've got lots to do with the funeral arrangements."

Jason grabbed a couple of mugs of coffee. Tiffany followed him into his well-appointed office. A triple set of bookcases housed what appeared to be an extensive library. A large walnut desk was the focal point, and there was a black leather sofa along with two occasional chairs. Tiffany sunk into the sofa, sipping her coffee.

"I'll call the funeral parlor, Tiffany. I know this is going to be hard for you. If you trust me, I'll take care of everything."

She caved in emotionally then. Tears cascaded down her cheeks. "Oh Jason, I don't know how I could have survived this without you." Her sobs bordered on hysteria, her emotions like a dam that had suddenly burst open.

"I knew you had bottled up your emotions. Go ahead and cry. You've been through a terrible shock."

"Stop! They can't be dead! It's all a terrible mistake." Tiffany put her hands over her face, sobbing, hysterically.

The sound of a wailing baby assailed her, jarring her

to her senses. Instantly, she was jolted back to reality. "Donnie is crying."

"Tiffany, my sweet girl, it really has been Donnie that has kept you sane. I believe God brought that baby into your life because he knew how desperately you would need him."

Tears clouded her eyes. She couldn't turn them off. Finally, after some time, she began sniffling. "Nothing will ever be the same again. I...relied on Dad for every business decision...and...Mom for emotional support...she's been there through all the ups and downs of my life...the broken romance with Lance...every crisis I've ever gone through. *How can I go on without her?*

"No...no...no...no!" Finally, she collapsed onto the leather sofa, emotionally spent. Jason moved toward her. "Tiffany, my darling girl, I'll walk with you through this. You don't have to face this alone. God has brought us together.

She sat on the sofa sobbing. Jason pulled her to her feet and held her close to him. She could feel his breath. His nearness snapped her out of it. He affected her in new and exciting ways. *She had never felt anything like this before. All she could feel, hear and sense was him. Everything else seemed to fade into the distance.*

Excitement screamed through every fiber of her

being. She was fully alive for the first time in her life. The emotions she felt were so deep and powerful, she thought she might explode. Minutes later, she felt like leaping and dancing for joy.

He kissed her then. His lips came down on hers, gently at first and then more intensely. She felt his burning passion for her. It matched how she felt. He seemed to be trying to restrain it. Unsuccessfully. She sensed it took every ounce of his restraint as he pulled away." I...I'm sorry. I don't know what came over me."

"Don't be sorry, Jason. I need your comfort and strength now like I need air." She couldn't let him go - wouldn't let him go. He was every man to her, the answer to her every need.

He pried himself loose from her. "We...have work to do," he said, resolutely.

"You're going to all-right, Tiffany. You've been through some high drama in the last couple of weeks. Try to relax. Your folks are with the Lord. They're in a better place. I believe God sent *me* to look after you and Donnie. Do you believe that?"

"Oh yes... I do believe that."

Somehow, Jason made the necessary calls and all the arrangements, while she sat numbly nodding and mumbling the odd, lame comment.

"So, it's all arranged for Friday. The reception will be in the church right after the funeral service. It all happens in three days."

Maria spoke through the closed door. "Hey guys, I made some fresh coffee. How is it goin' in there?"

Jason opened the door. "Your timing is superb as always, Maria."

"I think Donnie missed you." She had brought the stroller with her. He sat in it, fussing and squirming.

"Hey, Handsome," Tiffany cooed. She scooped him up. "You're getting used to your stroller, daren't you, darling? You look adorable. Hello Sweetheart," she said, holding him close.

Gradually, her breathing became even again. She glanced over at Jason, then gazed adoringly at Donnie. "You know what? I'm gonna be just fine."

"Coffee smells good," Jason said.

The aroma filled her nostrils, as she wheeled Donnie toward the kitchen. Maria had already moved into it. *A good cup of coffee would hit the spot.*

Jason followed her into the kitchen. Tiffany admired the gourmet kitchen, with its State-of-the-Art stainless steel appliances and honey-bisque, tiled floors. Maria handed her a mug of the fresh brew. She plunked down on a bar stool next to the granite counter. "Perfect," Tiffany said, after taking a sip. She parked Donnie's stroller next to her.

She was starting to calm down. *Somehow she would make it through this bleak valley.* Her new friends would be instrumental in that. Her girlfriends had both left messages on her cell, but she felt no urgency to return their calls. *Where had they been in her darkest hour?* She knew the answer to that - partying and soaking up the rays in Florida. God, in His love and wisdom, had not let her down. Jason, Maria and her Christmas miracle had become the central players in her life. She blew a kiss to Donnie. He smiled and gurgled up at her.

When God closes one door, he often opens two new ones. She remembered the classic prose about how God carries us through our darkest hour. He certainly did that for her. Her cell rang. She glanced at the call display. Tracey's number flashed on the screen. She might as well answer it. She needed to invite her to the funeral. She clicked a button. "Hey Tracey, what's goin' on?"

"The question is - what's goin' on with you? When is the funeral?"

"Friday at 10:00. I'll text you with the details."

"I'm so sorry this happened, Tiffany. You must be devastated."

"You got that right. Pass the word about the funeral to Jody, will you?"

"You got it."

She turned to Jason. "That call was well-timed. When you tell Tracey, word travels like wildfire."

Maria puttered in the open-island kitchen. She glanced out the window." That snow is really comin' down. I hope everyone will be able to make the funeral. When is it?" She glanced at Jason.

"Friday at 10:00. St. Paul's chapel on East 62nd street. And now, Ladies, if you'll forgive me, I need to take care of some of my business. I'll be in my office," he said, taking his mug of coffee with him.

"Why don't you have everyone come here after the funeral? I'll serve sandwiches and refreshments." Maria glances over at Tiffany.

"You would go to all that trouble for me? You hardly know me." A scripture flashed into her mind." *I was hungry, and you fed me. I was thirsty and you gave me something to drink...if you do it unto the least of these, you do it unto me."* Jason's voice took on a serious tone. "Somebody's got to take care of you, Tiffany. Between the trauma you've suffered and taking care of Donnie, you have your hands full. The Good Lord put us into your life for that very reason." Her eyes twinkled. "I think He likes you."

Tiffany smiled in spite of herself. *Did* God really like her? "Well, I'm a work in progress. I meditate on the scriptures every chance I get. Dad taught me that God is a rewarder of those who diligently seek Him. One of my favorite scriptures is "*If you delight yourself in Me, I will give you the desires of your heart."*

"I love that scripture," Maria said.

"I've wanted children ever since I was young. Instinctively, I sensed that I might not be able to have them. So, I took extensive tests with my doctor. Unfortunately, he confirmed my fears. He said that medically I could not have children. He...explained why, but I was so overcome with emotion, that I barely remember a word he said."

"We'll pray for a miracle...that you will be able to keep Donnie. Don't forget, Tiffany, *With God all things are possible.*"

"I must tell you, Maria. My ex-boyfriend, Lance vanished from my life when I told him that news. I hope I don't lose Jason. I couldn't bear another disappointment. Maybe I'd be smarter to end it before I get in any deeper."

"You really don't know Jason very well, Tiffany. And how could you? You've only just met him," Maria said. "He's one in a million, I'll tell you that much."

"But Maria, the man loves children. That much is obvious. There's no future for our relationship."

"Don't borrow problems, Tiffany. *Let each day's evil be sufficient unto itself.* Real love is about selflessness. *Isn't that what Christ was all about?*"

Tiffany hugged Maria." Yes, that's precisely why I should step aside and give Jason a chance to find a woman that would fulfill all the desires of his heart."

"Leave that up to Jason, Tiffany. He's a big boy and he knows what he's doing. Trust his judgment and trust the Creator. It's all going to work out; you'll see."

"Oh Maria, thank-you. You've been just wonderful. My girlfriends are nowhere to be found. Funny how even the persons you think are your best friends, might vanish when you need them most."

"It's a bitter lesson I had to learn, also. My closest girlfriend vanished when my husband died. When I needed her most, she deserted me. I learned then that the only one we can count on is the Lord. Only He got me through the trauma of losing my husband so...suddenly and... horribly."

"Maybe Jason and Donnie are merely loans to help me in my time of sorrow. I sure hope that I'm not about to lose both of them? *Lord, I couldn't bear it.*

Jason's long stride reached the kitchen. As if reading her thoughts, he brought up the issue that had been niggling at her. "Tiffany, I know you've been through a devastating loss - but I've always believed in addressing issues, sooner than later. I've learned that if you allow a situation to escalate, it becomes increasingly difficult to deal with."

"You're talking about Donnie, obviously. Right?" Tiffany asked.

"I am. I have to tell you, he's gotten under my skin, too. I understand how you feel, but we shouldn't wait another minute to report this to the authorities. I do not think Donnie should be present at the funeral on Friday. If he is, there are going to be a lot of questions you won't want to answer. I'm sorry, really sorry... but it's the next problem we need to tackle."

She choked back tears. *Oh Lord, why is life so difficult? No, I won't have a pity party.* Tiffany began counting her blessings. "Jason, you and Maria have become my earthly refuge from the storm. I leaned on the Everlasting Arms and he saw fit to thrust y'all into my life. Thank-you, Lord."

"We better start with the police. I'll tell them you were so traumatized that I was worried if I phoned them as soon as I knew about it, you might go off the deep end. You were so fragile...you still are."

She took a long sip of the coffee. "I'm sure you're right. Delaying the call will only make it worse. As it is, I have a lot of explaining to do."

"So, it's back to your office," Tiffany said.

"Yes. We need to report this to the police right away."

"So, we should forget about lawyers right now?"

"I think reporting the find to the precinct is a good place to start."

"Lord, strengthen and encourage Tiffany as she makes that call." Maria flashed her a warm smile.

"Thanks, Maria . You're such a...generous spirit."

"Hey, I just lost my husband three years ago to a massive heart attack. I know what trauma is. If I had been there at the time, I would have asked God to raise him from the dead...and I would have believed Him for it...but I wasn't there."

"I'm sorry. Where were you when he died?"

"Puerto Rico ... visiting my sister. Santos was alone in our apartment in New York. The coroner told me he was here one minute and with the angels the next. It was instant. So, you see, my dear, I just want to help others as much as I can. I believe that is my mission in life."

"I'm so sorry about your loss."

"Thanks. I never would have made it without Him." She pointed upwards.

"Come on, Tiffany, let's get this over with." Jason motioned for Tiffany to follow him to his office. She pulled Donnie close to her and kissed him on a cheek. He squirmed, giggling. "You little rascal. I love you," she said, before setting him back into his stroller and pushing him down the hallway to Jason's office.

Jason opened the office door and watched Tiffany wheel the stroller into it. "I ...I just want him near me when I make that call..." Tiffany said.

"I understand."

"What...should I say?"

"Don't lie to them. Tell them exactly what

happened."

Jason found the non-emergency number on the internet, scribbled it on a notepad and handed it to her. "There you go. You have nothing to hide. Just tell them what happened."

She was shaking as she dialed the police. A woman answered on the third ring. "Police. Non-emergency," the operator said, in a sleepy, hoarse monotone.

"I...have to report...finding a baby in an alley...in a garbage bin..."

"Just a minute, Ma'am," she said, in the same dull monotone. A moment later, she was back on the line. "*A garbage bin, did you say*?"

"Yes, Ma'am, that's what I said."

"No kiddin'." Her voice rose in alarm. "I'll have an officer call you right back."

Minutes later, the phone rang. "Sg. John Scott here. I'm going to need you to come down to the station and file a report. We'll match it with a search for any reports of missing infants. We may want to get this on the news right away, Ma'am. Every year, usually around Christmas time... we get somethin' like this."

"People do crazy stuff over the holidays. But the mother may have come to her senses by now. She may want the baby back. Post-partum blues could cause a mother to abandon her baby."

"Really. Could it?" Her mouth responded but her

heart and brain were screaming *no, no, no! You can't have my baby! He's mine. He's everything to me...my whole life. I found him and I'm keeping him*!

Of course, she didn't say it. She kept her mouth shut. *Even a fool is thought wise if he remains silent.*

"Can you come in right away to file a report? We'll need you to bring the baby. We'll want to take some photos of him...and arrange for an orphanage for him."

Tears trickled down her cheeks. She took a deep breath. "Sure, sure...of course." She marked down the address, glancing over at Jason, distraught.

"Come on, let's go. Let's get this over with," Jason said, taking her by the arm.

She saw the strain in *his* face, and that surprised her. She handed Jason the slip of paper for the 19th Precinct in New York. Jason was on his cell to his driver. "Nick...good-morning. We need to go down to the police station to file a report. How soon can you pick us up?"

"Right away, Jason. I'll call you when I'm out front."

"Sounds good."

They rode in silence except for some whimpering on Donny's part. *Did he sense the upheaval in her? The uncertainty of his own future? How much did babies perceive?*

"Good morning, officer," Jason said, as the three of them entered the reception area at the 19th precinct.

"We'll be right with you," the officer said. "Have a seat."

A woman arrived momentarily and ushered them into a room." A police officer will be right with you."

A few minutes later, an officer appeared. "I'm Sgt. Tripper. You must be Tiffany Vandermeer."

She nodded, numbly. "My friend, Dr. Jason Wilcott."

Start at the beginning, Ma'am. How and where did you find the baby?"

Tiffany relayed the events, shaking, as she relived it.

"I'm sorry to inform you of this, but we have had a woman contact us, identified as Louise May Stuart residing at an address near where you discovered the infant..."

Numbness swept through her like a chill wind. *Her worst fears were being realized." That which I have greatly feared has come upon me."*

"Apparently, the woman had a fight on the phone with her boyfriend. He threatened to harm the baby. She phoned 911 but he was banging on her door so hard she thought it might break. She slipped out the fire escape in the back and stashed the baby in the garbage bin. She was running for help when he spotted her. When he asked where the baby was, she told him he was in the hospital, and she was on the way there."

He got nasty and pushed her into his car. That's when she prayed for a miracle.

"I guess if you believe in the guy upstairs, you were led to rescue this infant and care for it, until his Mom could get her act together," the officer said.

"So...she wants him back..." Tears rolled down Tiffany's cheeks.

"Yes, Ma'am. I'm afraid she does. Matter of fact, she's waitin' in a room down the hall, to identify him."

Tiffany's mouth moved but no words came out. A paralysis threaded its way through her entire being.

"I guess we might as well get this over with, Honey," Jason said, peering at Tiffany.

The compassion reflected from his eyes touched her somewhere deep inside. "Yes, I guess we might as well..." Her voice seemed to come from the end of a long tunnel. Was she whispering? Was it actually her voice?

Constable Rolands disappeared, returning in minutes with a wispy, young woman. She was perhaps twenty, maybe younger. She was wringing her hands and kept apologizing. "I'm...I'm sorry I did this, I'm sorry. I'm sorry I didn't call sooner, I..." She glanced over at Donnie and frowned. "That's not him. That's not my baby." She turned and fled from the room, sobbing. Constable Rolands ran after her. The door was open so Tiffany could hear the Constable trying to calm the young woman down.

Tiffany began to breathe again. *Thank-you,*

Lord...and, please help that...fragile young woman to get her baby back!

The constable returned." Even if this little guy had been her baby, she wouldn't have been allowed to keep him. Criminal charges would need to be filed against her. If she had left him at a hospital or licensed adoption agency, she wouldn't be prosecuted. Those are considered safe places. But that's not where she put him."

"What about Post-partum blues? Aren't there allowances made for that?" Tiffany asked.

"Not legally. The best thing for you to do right now is to just keep the baby. I'll let you know which orphanage the baby will need to be dropped off at. If we do hear from the Mother, she will be prosecuted, and criminal charges will be brought against her."

"What about...if the baby's life was being threatened, and his Mom stashed him in the garbage can as a safety measure, albeit a desperate one?"

"Well, then I guess a good attorney would get the charges dropped and maybe she would be able to keep the baby. That isn't likely to happen. We usually hear something in the first forty- eight hours of abandonment."

"Thanks for the information," Tiffany found her voice, as a thread of hope filtered through her.

CHAPTER SEVEN

Tiffany awakened to the ring of her cell phone. Glancing at the call display, she recognized the number of the 19th Precinct. "Constable Jennings here. We have an orphanage lined up for the baby. I'll give you a phone number. You'll need to make an appointment."

"Thank-you," Tiffany said, feeling faint.

"I'd like you to call first thing this morning, if you would. It's probably best that you don't keep the baby any longer than is necessary. Every day that goes by makes it harder for the two of you to separate."

Her first thought was to run away. *"Ya, right. The funeral was tomorrow. So it would be like a double funeral. Her parents and Donnie - both being wrenched away from her. A final goodbye to all of them. Oh Lord, help me to go on.*

Her cell chirped. A glance at the screen told her it was Jason. It was as though he had heard her silent pleas. Shaking, she answered it, her voice trembling. "Oh Jason, the constable just called. They want me to drop Donnie off at the orphanage. I can't bear it. I just can't." Her eyes filled with tears.

"I'll be with you every step of the way, Honey. As a matter of fact, when the funeral is over, we're flying to Florida for a mini-vacation."

"We are? Gee, thanks for letting me know. What about your job as a doctor?"

"I'm taking an emergency leave of absence...just for a week. You're going to need all the emotional support you can get."

"B...but I..."

"I know...you don't want to travel...just the two of us. As it happens, Maria loves Florida. She's been there with the family many times. She'll be joining us."

"Ah. A chaperone. Where are we going? I mean, it's not as though I have any say in the matter." As she spoke, a thrill coursed through her. *A vacation in sunny Florida with Jason. Wow!*

"Longboat Key - a beautiful stretch of beach in Sarasota. White sandy beaches...balmy, warm weather. We own a house there. It's been in the family for more than a generation. "

"Really? You...never mentioned it before."

"I know. I guess I didn't think it was important."

"Thank, you, Lord. "One day at a time, sweet Jesus, that's all I'm asking from you..." The lyrics rang in her head and heart. She made the dreaded call immediately, before she lost her courage; and then called Jason back. "Would you pick me up around 9:00?"

They drove to the orphanage. Tiffany thought she was going to be sick. The three of them sat in the back seat of the limo. "I...can't do this, Jason," she said, as she gazed down at the innocent, unsuspecting infant cradled in her arms.

"We don't have a choice, Tiffany. We'll just keep praying for a miracle...that somehow we'll get him back."

Nick pulled up in front of a sprawling, ancient two story house. "It's okay, Tiffany. We'll get through this," Jason said, as they climbed the stairs to the front door. Tiffany held Donnie, as he whimpered. *Did he sense what was about to happen?* They rang the bell and waited. After a few minutes, a mature, somewhat regal and handsome woman, greeted them at the door. She smiled warmly. Her face was tanned and weather beaten as though she had lived most of her life outdoors in a sun-drenched area. Her platinum-grey hair was pulled back into a big, gold clip. Intense grey eyes studied them.

"Good-morning," Jason said. "I'm Dr. Prescott, this is Tiffany Vandermeer. We have Donnie with us."

"Please come in. I'm Estelle Davies, Director of the orphanage. I'll need you to sign some papers. Follow me." She led them to her office, gesturing for them to be seated. She pulled out a form from her desk, handing it to Tiffany.

"I'll take Donnie," Jason told Tiffany, "So that you can fill out the paper work." Jason held the baby. He started howling, bordering on hysteria.

Tiffany collapsed onto the sofa. With shaking hands, she filled out the forms. She touched Jason's arm, drinking in his strength. But as she glanced up at him, she saw that he, too, was broken-hearted about her having to sign Donnie away.

She handed the completed application back to the woman and picked up Donnie." Good-*bye, my darling, I'll be praying that God will return you to me,"* she whispered. Her entire body trembled. The baby sensed her mood, and began wailing again. Then, she did the hardest thing she ever had to do- she handed Donnie over to the matron. Her heart felt like it was ripping out of her chest. She couldn't breathe.

Putting an arm around her, Jason guided her back to the limo and helped her into it. She was numb as they drove back to his home. He helped her into the house. Maria greeted them, and gathered Tiffany into her arms. "I'm praying you'll get him back, dear. He has great and mighty things in store for you. You'll see," Maria said.

"I...hope you're right." She was fighting to be stoic.

"Lean not on your own understanding. In all your ways acknowledge Him and He will direct your paths."

"Thanks."

"Remember, Tiffany. His ways are not our ways."

"I...guess I need to pack a bag if we're going South."

"Don't bother - we can shop when we get there. You won't need much...a couple of bathing suits and lounge outfits for relaxing. Maybe some jeans and T-shirts." She snuggled against Jason's chest, emotionally exhausted, as Nick drove them to the airport.

The waterfront beach house was ancient and rambling. It was loaded with character. She marveled at the sweeping ocean view and pristine white sands. The smell of the sea air assailed her nostrils, as she stepped out of their rented Toyota Camry and walked with Jason up the few steps to the backdoor entrance. A tall Palm tree flanking one side of the house swayed in the breeze. Flourishing vegetation lined the back and front of the house. "Birds of Paradise! My absolute favorite. Oh, let me smell them. They're glorious." *Thank-you Lord, for bestowing this wonderful blessing on the heels of the sorrows."* She loved the scent and beauty of tropical vegetation. Jason was right. It was precisely what she needed.

Jason ushered the two women into the mansion. "Wow, what a great, old house this is!" Tiffany enthused.

"Glad you approve, Tiffany. Maria, please show Tiffany to a guest room. I'm going to check everything around the house and make sure it's all in working order. The house has been unused for some time. It was leased for the summer and my agent assured me she did a walk-through and it all looked good, but still, it's kind of a routine of mine whenever we visit here."

"Thanks, Jason," Maria said. "Follow me, Tiffany." Maria climbed the staircase, Tiffany close on her heels. She opened the door to a spacious guest room, sparsely furnished. A four-poster Mahogany bed with a canopy over it was the room's central point. She glanced at her reflection in the mirror while admiring the vintage antique dresser. The room was decorated in a tropical floral pattern, predominantly lime green and pink. The sea-green walls were dull and the paint was peeling in places.

She stepped toward the French doors, opening them. They opened onto a deck, revealing a sweeping ocean view. "Oh...oh...oh...oh...oh. What a magnificent view!" Her eyes swept the vast shoreline. Spun white sandy beaches stretched out below as far as the eye could see.

The house was ideally situated on a prime piece of real estate. It hardly took a real estate agent to figure that out. "Was this house one of the first houses to be built along this...magnificent stretch of beach?" Tiffany asked.

Maria smiled. "That's an astute observation. Mrs. Prescott told me this house was one of the original mansions built on the oceanfront here in Longboat Key. Of course, there's been a building boom along the oceanfront in the last fifty years or so. Now, there are dozens of newer homes along this shoreline."

On either side of the house, pristine, white sands stretched for miles. She watched the ocean crest and fall, mesmerized by the surf rhythmically lapping against the shoreline." Maria, this is the most exquisitely beautiful place I have ever seen in my life."

"I'm so glad you share my view."

A sandpiper landed on the deck. *Oh Lord, this little slice of heaven is exactly what I need. How could Jason have known?* She turned then, realizing Maria had quietly slipped out of the room, giving her a chance to embrace her new surroundings and familiarize herself with it. She didn't know how long she had been sitting on the white wicker chair on the deck, when she heard Maria's low, rich voice. "Hey, Tiffany, I'm making a pitcher of iced tea. Will you have some?"

"I'll be down in a few minutes," Tiffany said. She

was curious to see the walk-in closet. She walked into it, glanced around, marveling at the extensive built-in shelving for shoes and accessories. She hung up the two outfits she had brought with her and tucked her sporty tops into the top drawer of the dresser. The white cotton stretch pants and navy-and-white nautical cotton sweater had been comfortable to travel in, and it was perfect for now. She took off her brown, sporty travel shoes and pulled on a pair of white sneakers and hurried down the stairs to the kitchen, overjoyed by being here.

"There's a couple of things that need fixing but it can wait. We need to go grocery shopping. Who wants to do it?" Jason glanced from Tiffany to Maria.

"I'll take the car and go shopping. You two enjoy your time together," Maria said.

"That's what I thought you'd say. But, Maria, you have two weeks' vacation coming. Why don't you take this as one of your weeks and enjoy yourself. We can take care of ourselves. You know I love concocting new dishes. This will give me a chance to experiment. And there's always the barbecue."

"You Rascal. You love surprising people, don't you?" Maria broke into a wide smile. "Okay, I'm heading for the beach. Doesn't take much prodding to get me to play a Princess."

Jason grinned at both the woman. "Yeah, I do." Life

ain't always fun, so you gotta add some humor and spice every chance you get."

"You would know that...being a doctor," Tiffany said, shooting him a glance. *Perfect. He likes cooking and I'm a lousy cook. It's match made in heaven.*

"Maria, I want you to treat this holiday as *your* holiday, also. Not just *ours.* We can barbecue when I'm not inventing a new dish. I'm sure Tiffany won't mind throwing a salad together."

"You're spoiling me rotten. I love it. Hang onto him, Tiffany. You'll never find one like him, again. Well, bye for now. I think I'll go for a stroll on the beach," Maria said. "I'll just get my keys. Have fun shopping."

Maria smiled mischievously, offered an affected wave befitting a queen before flitting by them, snatching up her purse and heading out the door.

"I had no idea what fun Maria is." Tiffany smiled at Jason. She was starting to relax.

"She's the best. She's been with the family a long time. She's seen us through all kinds of stuff. She was there when I graduated from high school...she's part of the family."

"So did her hubby work for your family, also?"

"Yes, he was our chauffeur and gardener. Not that we have much garden in Manhattan. Anyway, they shared the suite downstairs. Yup, it's been over twenty years since they first started working for us."

"No wonder she *seems* like family. She *is* family."

"Yeah. She mothers me a lot. Mom moved to California when I was only fifteen. My folks separated. Mom hired Maria to cook and run the household. She rarely visited us. Maria has been a kind of surrogate Mom. Dad became ill, so I stayed on at the house right through Med school. I helped look after him until his fatal heart attack."

"Well, I guess it proves once again that God blesses us, despite the curves life throws at us."

"Maria wants to see me married and settled." He winked at her.

Tiffany stared at him. He was so handsome. She melted at the mere sight of him. He was such a hunk. *Would God ever bless her with a man of this caliber?* "And...how do *you* feel about that?"

"I was a confirmed bachelor...until I met you."

"Oh come on," she said, nervously. "A...great guy like you...you must meet attractive women everywhere you turn."

"I do meet a lot of good-lookin' women...but never one that set my heart racing like you do..." He peered at her then, as a serious expression stole over his features. "After the lawsuit with Brianna, I swore off women. I...became somewhat jaded, I guess."

"But now you're willing to try again?

"Some days, yes - some days, no."

She took a sip of the iced tea. "Maria makes great iced tea."

"Yes, she does. Ready to go grocery shopping?"

"Sure. I'll just go grab my purse."

Tiffany whisked up the stairs and into her room and snatched her designer purse from the bed and bounded down the stairs. "Let's go, Jason."

Jason opened the door of the Toyota. She stepped into it. "It's so amazing being here in the sunshine. Oh, Jason, thank you for bringing me here. God is so faithful. Even though he allowed my parents to move into the heavenly realm, and Donnie to be snatched away from me - I get to be in this sunshine Paradise with you! I stand in awe of Him."

Tiffany tried to remain strong. Leaning on the Everlasting Arms was helping her. "Oh Jason, I hope Donnie will be okay. Do you think I have a chance at adopting him?

"With God all things are possible, Tiffany. Lord knows I'll do everything I can to help you." He winked at her. "Your chances would probably increase if you were married... to a pediatrician." He grinned over at her.

"A man whose family was Old New York establishment, perhaps?"

"Something like that." His grin widened.

They drove along the coast. She marveled at the

grand ocean-front homes lining the pristine, white sandy shores. The weather was idyllic. "I need to marry a man who is willing to adopt children, since I can't have them. I know you love children...I can tell by the way you related to Donnie...not to mention your choice of occupation. I like you a lot, Jason, but we both know it can't go anywhere. In fact, after we get back to New York...maybe we should go our separate ways, before we become more deeply involved." Tiffany peered out the window trying hard to be stoic.

"Hey Tiffany. What happened to living one day at a time and leaning on the Everlasting Arms? We've bonded, honey. You can't deny that reality."

"That's exactly why I have to end it. You've become...everything to me...my closest friend and confidant. If we don't go our separate ways after this vacation, it will only become more difficult to end it, as time goes on."

Jason was silent, his eyes on the road.

She marveled at the spectacular houses lining the beach, visible from the main road running through Longboat Key. They drove for several miles, heading to the supermarket. Soon the opulent homes gave way to upscale condo properties with golf courses stretching for miles along the ocean. It was a blissfully perfect day - tropical and balmy. She couldn't ask for more.

Jason pulled the car into a crowded lot adjacent to a

marina and a seafood restaurant. He walked around the car and opened the door for her. Herons and a smattering of exotic, long-legged birds meandered around, as they stepped out of the car. A Pink Flamingo stopped in front of her peering directly at her, as if to say, "Humph...another tourist!"

"You know your way around here, I see," Tiffany said.

"Yep. Been comin' here since I was a kid. The food is very good here."

Minutes later, they were seated at a booth overlooking the ocean at the marina. "Any food we have left over from lunch, we usually give to the birds," Jason said. "That's why they all line up outside on the deck. They're waiting for their dinner. Some of the customers feed them directly. It's great fun."

"The tropical birds are magnificent!" Tiffany said. "What is that strange looking bird over there," she said, pointing to a particular, long-legged bird strutting on the boardwalk opposite their table."

"That, my dear, is a black-hooded Parakeet."

"Really? Look - it appears as though he's dancing with another Parakeet!"

"He is. They have elaborate, noisy courtships in which they actually dance together."

"No kidding! How romantic...and exotic!"

Jason smirked. "God made nature interesting.

Humans are fearfully and wonderfully made, and so are birds... and everything else on the planet."

"It's amazing that some people can look at all this and still believe there is no God. They gamble with their eternity." Tiffany said.

"I see it every day. Working at the hospital, I meet a lot of folks who know their time is short and yet still, they do not seek Jesus. I guess it would be like me offering you a gift, and you saying that you don't want it, and throwing it away. Jesus died a savage death so that we could live forever in His presence. He has promised a place so glorious and magnificent, that we do not even have the capacity to imagine it. I mean, it boggles the mind, what God has in store for us." Jason said.

"You're preaching to the choir...or maybe you're practicing to become a minister." Tiffany smiled. She reveled in his company.

"I think I'm just sharing my views with someone very special." He grinned at her, his eyes sweeping over her appreciatively.

Jason's cell chirped, interrupting their romantic lunch. He didn't bother checking to see who was calling. Instead, he leaned toward her. "You're very beautiful, Tiffany. Someday you will have beautiful, special children."

She set down her iced tea. "No, I won't, Jason. I'm

unable to conceive."

"What...whatever do you mean?"

"Just what I said. Can't have 'em. Something's wrong with me...it's...oh, never mind. It's just something I have to live with and whomever I marry will have to accept."

"With God all things are possible."

"True. But right now this is a medical impossibility. As soon as I get back to New York, I want to start the adoption process with Donnie."

"You know I'll help you in any way I can. Donnie is very special. In the brief time I knew him, he stole my heart, too. So, I know how you feel. You know...there is another way to look at this."

"Which is?"

"For starters, I believe God gave you a Christmas miracle - Donnie - to balance out the horror of losing your folks. He never promised us a rose garden. Never said life wouldn't be difficult or devoid of challenges. If you look at this another way, God has opened the door for a relationship with a special baby, and I believe He will cause this adoption to come to pass."

A word aptly spoken is like apples of silver. "Thank-you, Jason. You know exactly the right words to say to warm my heart. I appreciate the encouragement." She rewarded him with a big smile.

A lanky, exotic bird hovered near their table, almost

as though he sensed they were leaving.

A waiter was within earshot. "Excuse me, Sir. May we have some take-out cartons?" Jason asked.

"Of course." The tanned waiter shot them a practiced smile.

Minutes later, he reappeared with two take-out cartons, placing them on the table. Jason scooped up the remainder of their dinners and brought it to the Pink Flamingo as he sauntered down the boardwalk. As Jason set the box of food down on the boardwalk, the Flamingo fluttered over to it, hovering only a couple feet away from them. The exquisite pink Sea bird arched his long, graceful neck, swooping down with his broad bill, swiftly snatching up the remains of the fish and gobbling it down.

Jason grinned at Tiffany. "Isn't this fun?"

"Everything is fun when you're around." The words spilled unbidden from her mouth. She hadn't meant to gush. "Tropical water birds are such a joy. I've always been a bird watcher. In fact, whenever I feel down, I think of the song *His eye is on the sparrow and I know He watches me.*

CHAPTER EIGHT

"This unexpected vacation is a blissful gift from heaven. Thank-you, Jason."

"My pleasure, I assure you."

He helped her put away the groceries." How does Bluefish sound for dinner?" He playfully shooed her out of the kitchen.

"It better be good," Tiffany teased. "Where is Maria? She's been gone a long time."

"She's a nature lover. She'll find her way back around dinner time."

"I think I'll change into a bathing suit and sunbathe on the deck."

"As long as you're out of my kitchen, you're good, Tiffany." He grinned at her as he began the dinner preparations. She swatted him playfully before she left. The heaviness in her heart was beginning to lift, but she was still mourning and knew she would be for some time.

She climbed the staircase to her room and pulled out her New International Version Bible. It was always the first thing she packed when she traveled. She drew all her strength from The Word. And she never needed it more than she needed it now.

Glancing out the long bank of windows overlooking the terrace, a well of sadness washed over her, heightening and receding like the ocean tide. Grief was something she had to live through, and only God could help her do that. *I shall lean on the everlasting arms of Jesus and just take it one day at a time.*

She changed into a pink bathing suit, plucking out a pink sun hat from her belongings which were now in the walk-in closet. She picked up her Bible and stashed a novel into her beach bag and headed down the stairs. *It was so nice to escape the bitter winter with new friends and an idyllic vacation. "Thank-you, Lord,"* she whispered.

She settled onto the wraparound deck, harkening to the surf and the cacophony of sounds emanating from a bevy of nearby Sea birds. Opening her Bible, she began to read. Lost in the joy and peace of meditating on the Word, time stood still. She didn't know how long she'd been here, reading and alternately sobbing and praying. Despite mourning the loss of her folks and Donnie, she wholeheartedly embraced the Creator's goodness.

"Are you joining us for dinner?" Jason popped his head around the corner of the wraparound deck. He'd obviously accessed it from the bedroom he was staying in.

Whoa. Did he look good or what? Broad shoulders burst from his white polo shirt. Navy Bermuda shorts showed off long, muscular legs. She caught her breath. *If only she could have children. Maybe she could hook up with him.*

"Weeping may remain for a night, but rejoicing comes in the morning." *Oh Lord, Jason brings me so much joy. Thank-you for bringing him into my life.* Closing her Bible, she rose from the chaise. "Yes, I'm coming for dinner. Thanks for not forgetting about me." She teased.

He stood close to her, towering above her. "As if I could forget about you," he said, grinning.

He was so near to her that the scent of his woodsy after-shave wafted into her nostrils. The tropical breeze blew the earthy scent her way. She glanced into his eyes, overwhelmed by the attraction she felt for him. Jason encircled his arms around her, pulling her close. "As if I could ever forget you..." His tone was pensive. "Tiffany, you darling girl," he murmured." You are so special to me. So very special..." His lips *came* down on hers with tenderness and passion.

She soared to another world. A world where there was only joy unspeakable, a place that must be somewhere near heaven. She felt as light as a feather and buoyant - as though she were about to fly into orbit.

She felt his passion, fueled by a love she was certain was there and matched by a love that had been escalating within her, blooming like emerging blossoms in Spring. No words were needed. She knew now that there was no turning back. He was the man for her and there could be no other.

After quite some time, he pulled away. "Tiffany, my darling girl, will you marry me?"

She was dumbstruck. She could only nod, knowing she had been waiting for him all of her life. There were no conscious decisions, just an inner knowing that this was the man for her- God's best. The man she was meant to be with. Tears trickled down her cheeks. "I can't, Jason. You know I can't. I can't give you children. I love you and I don't want you to miss out on that blessing."

"I want you to be my wife, darling," he said, putting his hand over her mouth, playfully. "Shush, honey. I told you before, *"With God, all things are possible."* Only believe..."

She wriggled out of his grasp. "I don't want you to be disappointed. Maybe God doesn't have that for me

- for us." *But even as she spoke the words, she wondered why her faith didn't match his.*

"I believe God withholds nothing from those who trust Him. *Psalm 18: 1-6* says If you have faith and do not doubt, not only can you do what was done to the fig tree, but also, you can say to this mountain. Go, throw yourself into the sea, and it will be done. If you believe, you will receive whatever you ask for in prayer."

"Jason, I respect your great faith. But my level of faith doesn't match yours. I can't ask you to walk down the aisle with me, knowing I may not be able to fulfill one of your greatest desires. That's not love. That would be the height of selfishness. If, for whatever reason, God does not perform a miracle in my body so that I can bear your children, you would eventually grow to resent me, perhaps regretting the marriage. I can't let that happen. I won't let that happen."

"So, you're turning down my proposal?"

She could see he was deeply upset. She was too. It took every ounce of courage she had to speak up. "I'm sorry, Jason. I'd rather hurt you now before we commit to marriage - than years down the road. I couldn't bear it if you became bitter and harbored resentment toward me."

"Have you ever heard the verse in the Bible that says Let each day's evil be sufficient unto itself? We are cautioned not to borrow tomorrow's trouble."

"Let's talk about it again after dinner," Tiffany said. *Did she have weak faith? His faith was powerful; but did he have enough faith for both of them?*

He took her hand leading her into the dining room. "Sit, I'll serve the dinner. I made Bluefish. I hope you like broccoli. I topped it with mozzarella cheese and baked it - and I made a surprise salad."

"I thought I was supposed to make the salad."

"That was only a figure of speech. I actually like preparing the entire meal."

"You like the whole presentation - like a chef."

"Pretty much."

"Where is Maria? Shouldn't she be back by now?" Tiffany asked.

"Good question. I looked up and down the beach and didn't see her. I tried her cell to tell her dinner was ready, but there was no answer."

"She's been gone since morning. I think it's odd that she's not answering her cell."

"Yes, it is."

As Jason pulled a chair out for Tiffany and she settled onto it, he had a change of heart. "Maybe we better find her before we eat," Jason said. "She should be back by now."

"Maybe we better head down the beach and look for her. She must have lost track of the time...or maybe her cell phone fell in the water...I don't know," Jason said.

"Sure. Let' do it. It's a beautiful night for a walk anyway," Tiffany said.

They strode along the beach enjoying the sound and drama of the surf. "Paradise. This is truly Paradise, Jason."

He stopped and his eyes traveled over her. "Maybe we could have the wedding here. At least we can be assured that Mother and Graham will show up. They can cruise over from Palm Beach."

"Didn't you hear a word I said, Jason? Read my lips. I can't have children. So, I can't marry you because it's..."

He put his hand over her mouth, his eyes dancing. "In God's world, all things are possible, if we only believe. I'm not taking no for an answer, just so you know."

He took his hand off her mouth and drew her close. The kiss was long and passionate. When they drew apart, her knees were weak, and she knew she could not resist him. The love she felt for him was stronger, more powerful than anything she had ever known, and it could only come from God. Only He could create two people, allow them to meet and bless them with this powerful connection-the kind of love that happens once in a lifetime. The words flowed from her, unbidden. "Yes, oh yes, my darling. I love you, I love you, I love you..." Tears of joy trickled down her cheeks. *The Lord giveth and the Lord taketh away, praise be the name of the Lord.* Her parents had been taken from her, and they were in the heavenly Paradise. She had been given the gift of new love. She was in an earthly paradise. "Thank-you, Lord," she whispered, overflowing with gratitude.

Maria was hurrying toward them. She came out of a house on the beach. "I...I'm sorry I'm late for dinner. I ran into old Mr. Philpott...Nathan. I spotted him on his deck and waved to him, he insisted on having me over for tea. I couldn't get away. He talked on and on, about losing his wife...he seemed so lonely. He just needed someone to listen to him... before I knew it, it was past dinner and just as I was about to call y'all, I spotted the two of you on the beach. I put the phone on silent because I really wanted to listen to what he said, so I could provide some meaningful solace. I'm afraid I lost track of time."

Jason thought quickly. "Invite him for dinner. Poor soul. He needs the company. Come on, let's all go over there and insist he join us. I haven't seen him in years. It will be good to talk to him. He's such an interesting man."

"It won't take much convincing," Maria chuckled.

In minutes, the foursome strolled the beach enroute for dinner at the Prescott beach house.

Jason served the dinner on the patio. Tiffany made the iced tea and brought it out, while Maria amused their guest. "I have a dessert surprise," Jason said. He was back in a jiffy with a tray containing four stemmed glass bowls with fresh blackberries and whipped cream.

"Dinner will be at my house tomorrow night, if y'all would like to join me," Nathan Philpott said. "Fina thrives on throwing dinner parties. Claims she gets bored, otherwise. My live-in cook is the best."

Jason glanced from Maria to Tiffany. "We've only got a few days left, girls. What do you think?"

"Sounds like fun," Maria glanced from Jason to their dinner guest, Nathan. After all, she was on holiday, and the more social it was, the more fun it was.

"Is her cooking anywhere near as good as mine?" Jason teased.

"You'll have to come over and find out." Nathan was delighted to reacquaint himself with old friends.

CHAPTER NINE

Fina served Jambalaya. Hawaiian music played in the background. It was her heritage after all, and most guests usually enjoyed it.

After dinner, Nathan took everyone on a tour of his work. A renowned artist, he worked in a variety of mediums. There were collages, sketches, elaborate oils and pastels of tropical scenery and the ocean; exotic Sea birds and portraits, character paintings of men, woman and children...his topics were seemingly endless.

"Your work is...just brilliant...amazing," Tiffany said. "Here...in Longboat Key, it must be incredibly inspiring for you. How long have you lived and worked here?"

"Well...let's see now." He seemed to be in deep thought as he reflected on the past.

His guests were studying various paintings. "I cashed in my stocks and sold my apartment in New

York...maybe fifty odd years ago. Bin paintin' up a storm ever since then. Matter-of-fact, this little slice of heaven...this idyllic paradise... has been my inspiration all these years. This... and Verena, my precious wife. I thank the Creator every day for the time I had with her...you know, I actually think God allowed her to transcend this world, so that I could spend more time drawing near unto Him....just one on one...used to be, that I thought I was too busy to seek Him. But everything changed...when Verena died. If there is an upside to her passing, it's that I have learned to lean on the Everlasting Arms."

"Well, Jason, do you think we should be heading home?" Tiffany pulled her eyes off a picture of a yacht on high, turbulent seas, glancing at him. This new world she had entered, filled with magnificent art, both inspired and heightened her insight. "I was thinking that we should have a small, impromptu wedding, right here at the beach... or maybe charter a yacht and have the wedding there. It would be so easy for Joanne and Graham to cruise over here from Palm Beach as you said."

Jason was stunned. Speechless. He could hardly believe his ears! *Was this really happening? Was this dream coming true? Was his most fervent prayer being answered? Would he return to New York with Tiffany as his bride?*

Maria was so excited she could hardly contain herself. She actually jumped up and down with overflowing glee. "One of New York's most eligible bachelors get's hitched! Wow! This is big. It will for sure hit all the social columns."

Joanne and Graham brought a video camera as well as a high-powered camera. A very small group assembled on the yacht which was only rented for one blissful, memorable day. Tiffany was dazzling in an exquisite white lacy dress, purchased off the rack. Jason wore a black tux. Joanne wore a stunning peach dress and hat. Graham was elegant in a light tan linen jacket, pin-striped shirt and co-coordinating slacks. Maria was the proud maid-of-honor in a new Lavender-colored dress. Tracy Hamilton and Jody White, her girlfriends, drove in from nearby Sarasota. Jason, Tiffany and their wedding guests dined on lobster, served with Cristal champagne.

"May I propose a toast to the bride?" Jason asked, a mischievous twinkle dancing in his eyes. Tiffany smiled joyfully. She was radiant. The guests reveled in the precious moments. "To the sweetest, most beautiful and charming lady on the planet...my precious wife. I love you with all my heart." He kissed the bride again.

Back in New York, Tiffany moved into the Brownstone with Jason, her new hubby, soon receiving her substantial inheritance. Due to Jason's persistent prayers and unwavering faith, she was finally persuaded to see a doctor and get a second opinion to determine whether or not she could get pregnant.

Before the appointment, Jason sat her down." Remember *Mark 11:23 & 24*. It goes like this: For verily I say unto you, That whosoever shall say unto this mountain, Be thou removed, and be thou cast into the sea; and shall not doubt in his heart, but shall believe that those things which he saith shall come to pass; he shall have whatsoever he saith. Therefore I say unto you, What things soever ye desire when ye pray, believe that ye receive them, and ye shall have them."

He spoke the scripture aloud every day for almost two weeks, Tiffany joining him, as instructed, while they waited for her doctor's appointment with the specialist. He believed that despite the diagnosis of her previous doctor, she would be able to conceive. They spoke the words aloud every day during that time, activating their faith: "The doctor will find nothing wrong with you. You will be able to conceive, Tiffany."

Jason accompanied her to the doctor and waited in the waiting room for the good news. It came.

He knew the minute she walked into the room. Her face was glowing, the joy, palpable. Tiffany threw her arms around him, radiant. "Oh Jason...the doctor couldn't find a thing wrong with me! He said I was either misdiagnosed in the first place... or a marvelous miracle has occurred!

As they hugged and celebrated the wonderful news at home, Tiffany rose from their embrace on the living sofa. "I'm going to make a pot of tea," she said.

Jason followed her into the kitchen. "What's on your mind, Tiffany? Something is bothering you."

She watched the kettle, waiting for it to boil. "Donnie is on my mind and heart. Jason...could we start the adoption process right away? I have no idea what is involved in adopting a baby, but I intend to find out." He put his arms around her. "What took you so long? I told you...he stole my heart too...he's a precious, special baby...let's pray right now that God will open the door for us to adopt him."

Right there in the kitchen, his arm around her, he prayed. "I know it will happen," he said, when they pulled apart from the embrace. I know, because God is a God of miracles. It is no accident that you found that baby before he froze to death, it was no accident that you met me in the drug store...none of it was an accident...and you'll see that this door...the chance to adopt Donnie will open."

The matron greeted them at the orphanage. "I'm sorry, Donnie was just adopted a couple of days ago," she said. "Please come in. Perhaps there's another baby..."

Jason cut her off. "Are you sure, Ms. Davis? I believe God meant for us to have him."

The matron looked at them strangely. "Well...the couple that adopted him...haven't actually picked him up yet...there are a few details to be taken care of first."

"May we see him?" Jason asked.

Tiffany was so overwhelmed by emotion that she could not speak. She was so grateful that Jason was doing the talking and the thinking...taking care of everything.

"Well...I don't know. I mean he *has* been adopted...and..."

The shrill cry of an infant broke into the momentary silence. It was nearby. "That's Donnie...I just know that's him..." Tiffany said, excited. She rushed toward the sound. The door to a large room was open. Several babies stood up in their cribs, holding the rails, peering at her. Jason was on her heels.

The matron hurried after them. "Mrs. Prescott...you...aren't really supposed to go in there...without my accompanying you."

Tiffany glanced over at the matron. She was struck by her countenance. It was soft, radiant, her eyes gentle. She looked stately with her platinum-grey hair pulled back with a clip.

"You love babies, don't you?" Jason said.

"So very much," the matron said, smiling. She stood next to the crib Donnie occupied, Tiffany next to her. "He's calmed down considerably."

"May I hold him?" Gentle tears, barely discernible, trickled down Tiffany's cheeks. In a kind of daze, she glanced over and realized Jason was standing next to her.

The matron nodded. Tiffany scooped Donnie up into her arms. "My precious, precious child," she said. "I've missed you so much." She kissed him on his cheeks and his face lit with recognition and joy.

"Take the baby and come into my office, please...both of you. I shouldn't really be doing this...but...well...sometimes mere men are not the authority. After all, God is the authority over all humanity, and in the end, he's the only one I'll need to answer to. I can readily see that you fill the void and are helping to heal from the emotional scar left by his abandonment. And I guess that's why I never felt any peace about giving the baby to the other couple. I really believe God wants you to have him. And if my conviction is correct, He will see it to fruition and the other couple will gracefully back off."

Soon, they were all seated in the matron's office, the door closed. "I knew in my heart that you two would be back. I prayed that you would adopt this special boy. I must tell you...the couple was nice enough that wanted to adopt him. They checked out beautifully and they completed the home study required for adoption, but I still knew in my heart that this child belonged to you. So I prayed. In my spirit I felt that I should not give Donnie to the other couple, despite their stellar background check. A few minor details needed to be worked out...so I postponed finalizing the adoption. I phoned them and said I had another little boy I thought would suit them better. His cultural background and physical characteristics were a better match."

"They were anxious to adopt, but nonetheless well-mannered busy professionals. They didn't press me on it. And then today...there you were...walking back into Donnie's life. I know it's a moment of destiny. I wish every adoption would culminate ideally like I believe this one will. I know that the two of you are meant to be his parents. But you do understand I'll need to phone the other couple and have a meeting with them, and get them to sign off on their interest in adopting him. The other baby should meld better into their family. After all, we don't know anything about Donnie or his heritage. So, if I can persuade the other couple to apply to adopt the other baby, and assuming they release their interest in applying to adopt Donnie, then he's all yours." The matron spoke with authority and conviction.

"I'll send the Home Study required for the adoption. Dr. Prescott, I'm sure it will be a breeze for you. And Tiffany, you're a born Mom, you'll take to the material, also."

She had never seen Donnie so happy. His startling, enormous blue eyes gaped up at Tiffany, his face lit with pure joy.

"You'll have to go through the process of course. That should move quickly. Dr. James Prescott, Jason's Dad was an anonymous donor of this private orphanage." The matron's eyes twinkled. "I've already done your background checks, because I knew you'd be back."

The matron smiled warmly at the Prescott's, handing them the adoption papers and the course. "We'll put Donnie back in his crib and I'll make a couple of phone calls. I shall do everything in my power to expedite the process, as well as persuade the other couple to focus their interest on William. I believe that baby is ideally suited for them."

The day they brought Donnie home was a joyous celebration. Tiffany, Jason and Maria were all ecstatic. That first night, as Tiffany snuggled up to her husband, having smothered Donnie with kisses, his gleeful giggles still playing in her ears, she glanced up him.

"Jason, what did I ever do to wind up with an awesome guy like you and a great kid like Donnie?"

"I don't know. But I bet God does."

The End

If you enjoyed Love Found in Manhattan, you may like Angel in Shining Armor

Made in the USA
Middletown, DE
14 March 2018